Author's Note

This story is set in the Stockbridge area of Edinburgh, Scotland. I ask that you forgive the liberties with dates. Stockbridge, earlier called Stockaree, was not established until the very early 1800s, which means that during our hero Padriag Clarre's time, it did not exist.

While researching a location for Padriag's home that would work for when the four knights set out on their original quest in the 1600s, Stockbridge was the best match, so I decided to use it.

AN UNLIKLEY KNIGHT

THE CURSED KINGDOM

HILDIE McQUEEN

USA TODAY BESTSELLING AUTHOR

All rights reserved.

No part of this publication may be sold, copied, distributed, reproduced or transmitted in any form or by any means, mechanical or digital, including photocopying and recording or by any information storage and retrieval system without the prior written permission of both the publisher, Oliver Heber Books and the author, Hildie McQueen, except in the case of brief quotations embodied in critical articles and reviews.

NO AI TRAINING: Without in any way limiting the author's [and publisher's] exclusive rights under copyright, any use of this publication to "train" generative artificial intelligence (AI) technologies and/or large language models to generate text, or any other medium, is expressly prohibited. The author reserves all rights to license uses of this work for the training and development of any generative AI and/or large language models.

PUBLISHER'S NOTE: This is a work of fiction. Names, characters, places, and incidents either are the product of the author's imagination or are used fictitiously. Any resemblance to actual persons, living or dead, business establishments, events, or locales is entirely coincidental.

An Unlikely Knight Copyright 2025 © Hildie McQueen

Cover art by Dar Albert, Wicked Smart Designs

Published by Oliver-Heber Books

0 9 8 7 6 5 4 3 2 1

Chapter One

VILLAGE OF CULROSS, SCOTLAND

The salty scent of the Firth of Forth drifted through the narrow streets, mixing with the rich aroma of ale and freshly baked bread from the nearby bakery. It was the kind of place where time moved slowly, even the cobblestone streets reminding of times past.

Erin Maguire had agreed, against her better judgment, to meet Tammie Lockhart at The Red Lion, a cozy pub with white-shuttered windows and a red brick façade that stood at the heart of Culross, a picturesque village an hour north of Edinburgh where she currently lived.

Meeting the petite blonde at the pub was a far better option than venturing to Dunimarle Castle, a place haunted by more than its centuries-old stone walls. To go there would bring stark reminders of the memory of something that made her question her sanity.

The idea that other realms existed, that travel between

them was possible, sounded just as absurd now as it had the day after she'd returned from what Tammie insisted on calling "the alter-world." No matter how many times she told herself what happened was impossible, no amount of logical reasoning could erase the fantastical things she had seen.

If not for the fact that the woman sitting across from her was unwaveringly insistent and could describe every last detail of what Erin herself remembered, she would have an easier time dismissing it all as a hallucination. A realistic dream caused by too many late nights reading fantasy romance novels.

There had to be a logical explanation. Shared delusions. Some kind of psychological phenomenon. She had read about those before, they were called collective hallucinations. If it weren't for the fact that pulling out her phone mid-conversation would be rude, she'd be researching it right now.

"We need your help," Tammie said again, her voice edged with desperation.

Erin exhaled a slow breath and leaned back in the booth, pressing her head against the solid wood.

"I'm trying to forget," she admitted, her voice barely above a whisper.

Tammie leaned forward, tapping her finger against the wooden tabletop with urgency. "I totally understand why you'd want to push the memory away. What happened was horrifying. But..."

"But?" Erin cut in. "You're saying that it's my responsibility to save Padraig, the man who is supposedly still trapped there?"

A flicker of frustration crossed Tammie's face. "Not supposedly. He *is* trapped there, Erin. And we desperately need your help."

We.

That single word carried the weight of an impossible truth. Tammie and her sisters had already rescued four men, knights who had been cast into that place centuries ago by an evil sorcerer named Meliot. The wizard had cursed them, banishing them to the alter-world after they thwarted his attempt to seize a village. For nearly three hundred years, the men had been lost in a strange enchanted realm, prisoners of dark magic.

It was the kind of tale that belonged in a book, not real life. Every part of it was as unbelievable as sprouting wings and flying to the moon.

Erin exhaled sharply. "What could I possibly do to help? You and your sisters actually know and understand magic. The closest I've come to anything remotely mystical is cracking open a fortune cookie."

A storm of thoughts whirled through her mind. She could refuse to help, put her foot down and make it clear she wanted nothing to do with this insanity. She could ignore Tammie's pleas, distance herself from the others who also insisted that it was real—that *she* had been abducted, taken to another realm, and barely escaped with her life.

Or ...

She could agree to help.

The thought sent a cold shiver racing down her spine. Her throat tightened, and she blinked hard against the sudden burn of tears.

If she said yes ... then what?

What if it was true?

And what if she was taken again?

The other realm had been a place like no other. Purple skies, more than one sun, extra moons as well. Live creatures and beings that should only exist in fantasy or horror movies. There had been a dragon, a huge fire breathing creature that had flown with the grace of a bird. Then there was the evil sorcerer, Meliot, who'd taken her captive and had nefarious plans for her. Erin had yet to find out what he planned for her, and she was more than fine with not knowing.

"Come to Dunimarle, let us tell you everything." Tammie's eyes searched hers. "Please."

Erin shrugged. "The last time I was there, you told me what you all believed to be true. I heard it all and considered what you asked. I don't think there is much else I need to know at this point."

"You were in shock still. We'd just returned from the alter world. You'd been unconscious, perhaps not well enough to understand everything."

"Knowing that I was unconscious proves to me that I must have imagined it all. Have you considered that you and I were drugged and somehow were misled?"

Tammie shook her head. "As I have explained, I am not the only one who has been there. My sister Sabrina has, too. Her partner Gavin, as well as the others, Tristan, Liam, and my Niall, were trapped there, with Padriag. Now he remains alone. It is imperative to save him before it's too late. Please Erin, if you can just try, I promise if it doesn't work, I'll stop insisting."

The angst in Tammie's eyes made Erin hesitate. "I am not sure what to do. A part of me wants to help. I really do, but I have to care for myself. My mental health and personal safety are my priority."

"I understand." Tammie blinked as if she fought the urge to cry. "I don't blame you. Hopefully we can find another way."

After paying for the untouched drinks, both stood and walked outside. Across the street, Erin caught a familiar sight that made her heart lurch. Tall, muscular, with midnight black hair, he looked to have stepped right out of a romance novel.

His name was Niall McTavish, and he was the man Tammie had supposedly rescued from the other world. At least, that is what she remembered. He lifted a hand in greeting, and she returned the gesture, hurrying to her car.

Pulling away, Erin caught sight of Tammie going to Niall and leaning against his chest, a posture of defeat.

"I can't do it. I won't do it." Erin repeated the words as her car turned a gentle curve in the road, leaving Culross behind.

AFTER DAYS of searching for a new place to live, she'd finally found one that sounded, and looked, too good to be true. Her current flat was cramped and noisy, much too close to a busy street. With Erin's lease ending, she'd given notice of moving. Time had quickly passed and, with only days before her lease was up, there was an urgency to find another home.

As someone who often allowed her heart to rule in making decisions, Erin enlisted the help of her cousin Aubrey, who had no qualms about giving her opinion and pointing out potential issues.

Their fathers were brothers, Erin's was the eldest, Aubrey's was second born. The brothers had married in the same year, both meeting their wives directly after settling into jobs.

Aubrey's father, an executive at an investment firm, married a beautiful woman from Ghana whom he'd met at the firm. Erin's father, who'd died from a heart attack, had been a solicitor and her mother a secondary school teacher.

"I love this place," Erin exclaimed, her spirits lifting at seeing the charming house with ivy cascading down one wall.

"The building is nice," Aubrey said as they stood shoulder to shoulder looking at the house which, according to the advertisement, dated back to the late fifteen hundreds. They had been instructed to make their way through an archway beside the house and enter from a gate on the side.

Aubrey led the way, sun glistening on her rich brown curls, that bounced with each step.

There were a few shallow steps before the two women came to the gate. Opening it, Aubrey motioned for Erin to go first, and they continued forward along a neat row of stepping stones that cut through a manicured garden.

"This place is adorable," Erin exclaimed, a smile stretching across her face.

Her cousin pushed a finger into Erin's upper arm. "Honestly though, you should reconsider moving in with me and not into another flat," she urged, referring to the large family home from which her aunt and uncle had recently moved, claiming to need a simpler life. That they'd moved into a larger home and taken most of the staff was amusing.

Erin gave her cousin a knowing look. "The house is too far from the city, the drive to and from the studio would eat up most of my day. From here I can walk. Plus, most things are within a couple miles. Market, bakery, pub ..."

Although she and Aubrey owned a thriving yoga studio there in Edinburgh, Erin taught classes and managed it, leaving Aubrey to hold yoga events in the villages closer to the family's estate

"Fine. Fine." Aubrey held up her hands. "Let's have a look, and then we should go to the pub after."

A woman of about fifty, with gray streaked hair pulled up into a messy bun, opened the door. Smiling widely, she motioned for them to enter. Erin liked her immediately.

In the small, open foyer, there was a table with fresh flowers, and not much else.

"You must be Erin," the woman said. "I am Julia. As you can see, the house has been separated into two flats, each with two bedrooms, a sitting room, kitchen, and dining area. The flats have a private patio and share the garden. Julia ushered them to a door and opened it.

Julia pointed to the opposite side of the building. "I live here but am only in the city half of the week. If you need anything, I will give you my number, or you can leave a note on the door."

As soon as Erin stepped inside the bright flat that was for

rent, her breath caught. The ceilings were high, which meant the windows were as well. Sunlight streamed through the French doors into the sitting room giving it a welcoming air. There was a good-sized kitchen, a small pantry, and a surprisingly large bedroom that could easily fit a queen size bed, dresser and her favorite overstuffed chair. The second bedroom was small, which would work well for an office or craft room.

"It is absolutely perfect," Erin turned in a circle. "I'll take it."

"We have other flats to see," Aubrey, the voice of reason, prompted. "We should go look at them before you make up your mind."

Julia and Erin exchanged looks. The woman seemed to understand she wouldn't change her mind. "I believe this flat is where you belong," Julia chimed.

Chills traveled up Erin's arms. It was a sign that she'd found her new home. She peered out the window, her back to the two women as a smile crept up her face.

"I don't need to keep searching. This is where I'm going to live."

Chapter Two

THE ALTER-WORLD

Padriag Clarre stalked from one side of his bedchamber to the other, his modern shoes barely making a sound. He'd not been outside in days, as Meliot, the warlock who'd trapped him there three centuries earlier, had wolf sentries surrounding the keep.

Centaur-like creatures also patrolled, their constant attention on the windows. When he dared peer out, they'd quickly notch an arrow and shoot it. Had to give them credit for their astounding accuracy. Padriag only dared to peek out fleetingly and then move away to avoid being speared.

How long had it been since he'd been in this world alone? Almost a year was his guess, ten months, thereabouts?

At first he'd been meticulous about marking each passing day, but now, at times, he'd forgotten if he'd done it and so he'd skipped days here and there. What did it matter? Ten months, or one more, time stretched, and it seemed like an eternity.

In the beginning of the curse, four others had been condemned to life in that magical, dangerous place with him. A severe punishment for saving a village from attack by a powerful wizard. Almost three hundred years later, his friends had been released from the curse one by one, recently rescued by true love.

After the first knight, Tristan McRainey, had been rescued, followed by the others, he'd fully thought his turn would eventually come. And yet, at times like this, when he was utterly alone with only silence for company, he admitted being jealous of their good fortune.

Other than occasional visits from Liam, a British knight who'd managed to keep his ability to travel between the realms, Padriag remained alone.

A part of him wanted to give up hope as the others had been released with only a short period between them. For whatever reason, his situation was very different; no matter how much the others tried to come up with a way to break his curse, it had yet to happen.

An aroma wafted past his open door, and he sniffed the air. Was it sausage he smelled?

Prepared for one of the wizard's tricks, Padriag picked up his sword and crept down the stairs, stopping every so often to listen.

When he was able to sneak a look into the main room, he lowered his sword. "Liam. I didn't expect to see you."

"I made a full English," the Brit said. "The best meal ever invented."

Padriag rolled his eyes. "I prefer a full Scottish."

"What's the difference?" Liam asked, "Lack of taste in the Scottish one?"

In truth, the food smelled delicious, but he couldn't keep from teasing Liam. "It's missing tattie scones."

"Eat," Liam said, motioning to the chair opposite him. "Tell me what has occurred of late."

"Since every day is the same here, you should tell me what happened on the other side," Padriag replied, pulling a chair out to sit.

While they ate, Liam informed him about the progress they'd been making in assuring Padriag's freedom. He barely listened. For the past months, nothing had worked. In fact, their efforts seemed to be doing more harm than good. Padriag was finding it harder to travel between the realms, perhaps mainly because going to Scotland was heartbreaking knowing that soon he'd be trapped in the alter-world forever.

"You must come to the other realm in a sennight. There is a spell they've been working on. John is convinced it could work," Liam explained, referring to his partner and the other knights' women.

"Could," Padriag said, his eyes flashing to the windows as a shadow crossed outside. "I will do my best to be there. Right now we must prepare. It seems either Meliot has sent something to spy on us, or perhaps I've acquired a pet dragon."

Both men hurried to the window and peered out, a flash of fire lighting the skies. Meliot's guards had scampered away, fearful of burning blasts that would scorch them instantly. In the sky, a familiar beast circled the keep, its huge wings moving with grace.

"That's Sterling's dragon," Liam murmured as the animal let out a loud eagle-like call.

A parchment floated in the air, landing just outside the door. Then, with one last cry, the magnificent beast flew away.

Padriag hurried to the door and opened it. After insuring there was no one about, he fetched the rolled parchment and went back inside.

He read over it and then read it again.

"What does it say?" Liam asked, eyes trained on the parchment.

"An invitation from Sterling to live in his realm until I am freed," Padriag replied. "It must mean Meliot has something bad planned, and the prince has heard of it. Where is Esland anyway?"

Liam let out a long breath. "I have never heard of anyone that has been there, but I know it borders the far side of Atlandia." The Brit almost looked excited. "It seems we are moving to Esland."

"We?" Padriag scowled at the Brit.

"I've always wanted to see it." Liam shrugged. "We best pack and be on our way."

Padriag stood. "Exactly how do you think we will get there? We don't have horses, remember, they're in the other realm."

Both stared at each other for a beat.

Padriag blew out a breath. "Why would he send the invitation without instructions of how we are to get there. We aren't even sure of where exactly it is."

"I am sure he has a plan." Liam was not to be deterred from going to what was purported to be a beautiful land.

Returning to his bedchamber, Padriag studied the items in his trunk. There wasn't much to pack. They'd not many belongings other than a few articles of clothing, leather boots, and weaponry. During his visits to the other realm, Padriag had collected a few pairs of jeans, a pair of pullovers and some underwear.

Since he didn't own a bag, he yanked a cover from his bed and folded it in half. Then he collected his belongings and neatly stacked them in the middle. After that, he folded the blanket over the piles and tied it all with a rope.

"I wondered how you would collect all your things," Liam said from the door. "What I want to see now is how you plan to carry it across the miles."

Padriag turned, giving his friend a triumphant smile. "You forget I retain my power of magic." Lifting his hand, palm up, he demonstrated as the bundled rose from the bed and floated in the air.

"It's too bad your magic can't transport us there," Liam said dryly.

Just then pounding sounded and the bundles of clothes fell clumsily onto the bed.

Both men listened intently to what sounded like a battering ram hitting the thick wooden front door.

Closing his eyes, Padriag ensured the protective ward was in place and did his best to make it stronger.

"The wards are holding," he told Liam, who scowled.

"We'd best figure out how to get out of here, because sooner or later, they will manage to get through."

Liam wasn't wrong. They shouldn't have been able to get that close to the keep, as Padriag had placed a perimeter of wards to keep them at a distance.

A horrible thought invaded his mind.

His powers were weakening.

Chapter Three

The bell over the door chimed softly as Erin stepped into Stewart's Books & Magic bookshop, the familiar fragrance of aged paper and vanilla-scented candles wrapping around her like a warm embrace. The shop was a charming retreat from the bustle outside, cozy and inviting, with tall, overstuffed bookshelves bowing under the weight of well-loved tomes. Tables showcased special editions, their gilded spines catching the light, and in the back, a snug sitting area with plush chairs beckoned customers to linger over a good read.

Behind the counter, John Murray glanced up from ringing up a customer, his bespectacled face lighting up as he spotted her. He lifted a hand in greeting before turning his attention back to the transaction. John was in a couple with Liam Murray, a British man who, according to Tammie, had also been trapped in the other realm.

Despite her initial hesitation about attending, she couldn't resist the pull of tonight's event—an intimate reading with one of her favorite local authors, Daniella McFadden. The prospect of hearing Daniella read in person had been too tempting to pass up.

She was early—nearly half an hour ahead of schedule—which meant only a few other guests had settled into the sitting area. The reading was limited to just fifteen attendees, ensuring an intimate, personal experience.

As she approached a table displaying Daniella's latest novel, *A Matter of Truth*, her gaze was immediately drawn to the mesmerizing cover. She lifted it to closer inspect the deep swirls of violet, crimson, and indigo blended together, creating a dreamlike effect, with three luminous moons suspended in the backdrop. The image made her chest tighten—an odd flutter of recognition of a place she'd been to.

The image was jarring to the point that she barely registered the book slipping from her fingers until it hit the edge of the table with a dull *thud*. Heart lurching, she managed to snatch it up just before it tumbled to the floor.

"You damage it, you buy it," John's teasing voice pulled her back to the present, his warm gaze twinkling with amusement. Of medium build, with tussled brown hair and clean-shaven face, he was the epitome of a handsome young Scot.

Erin forced a smile, her pulse still unsteady. "Guess that means I have no choice now, huh?"

John chuckled, then leaned in to press a light kiss to her cheek. "How are you, dear?"

"Good ... great." She struggled to form the words, her attention drifting back to the book's cover. "The cover. It's ... interesting, isn't it?"

John followed her gaze, nodding in appreciation. "It is, but I like it."

"Yes ... of course. Me too." Erin swallowed, her fingers tightening around the book. "I—I'll take this copy. I'd love to get it signed."

After she paid, John gestured toward the sitting room, his smile as warm as the shop itself. "Go get comfortable. I'll fix you a cup of tea."

Before long, people trickled in until every seat in the sitting room was taken. John was an excellent host, ensuring everyone had a beverage and a bite from the offerings of biscuits, scones, or fruit platters.

The bell over the door jingled, Tammie and her sisters, Sabrina and Gwen, appeared. Tammie had told her they were coming. Being they were considered family by John they'd purposely arrived later, so as not to take a seat from other attendees.

The sisters settled just outside the wide opening from the sitting room, Sabrina sinking into a reading chair, Gwen sat on the footstool, and Tammie dragged a tall chair from behind the counter and climbed onto it. She smiled brightly at Erin, who returned one of her own.

John stood in front of the room and held up both hands to get everyone's attention. The murmuring instantly ceased, every eye on him.

"Welcome. I am so pleased to see everyone. Daniella insists that you feel free to help yourself to more drinks and snacks while she's reading. This is an informal gathering." He went on to read the author's bio and then introduced the woman, who came down a stairwell.

Daniella McFadden was in her early forties, her dark brown hair, with a few sprinkles of premature gray, cut in a blunt long bob. Her face was devoid of any lines, a creamy complexion that most women could only dream of. Her brilliant green eyes were lined, the black liner slanting upwards on the outer corners, and her lips were painted a soft plum. Wearing a flowing dress made of different fabrics with contrasting patterns, dangling earrings and a multitude of bracelets, she was definitely boho chic.

Once the author settled, she scanned the room, hesitating on Erin for a moment, her brow lowering just a bit. The movement was so slight that Erin was sure the others in the room didn't notice, but when she looked over toward Tammie, the woman lifted a knowing eyebrow.

When Daniella began reading, the words flowed easily. It was obvious she was comfortable with the passage by the way she continued quoting while looking up every so often to glance at those gathered. The reading pulled Erin in, the words of a woman who tried to convince others of the possibility of other worlds existing.

Once Daniella finished reading, and asked for questions, a woman lifted her hand shyly. "How did you research for this book? I've already read the book and love it. Since obviously there are no other worlds, you have a brilliant imagination."

Daniella smiled at the woman. "Thank you. I spoke to multiple people who claim to have visited other realms. The description in this story is a merging of their descriptions. The interesting thing about this is that there were very few differences in the realms they described."

There were several more questions, even Gwen and Sabrina asked about muses and what lead to the book, but Erin couldn't keep from wanting to race out of the store to read the book. What if the world described in the book was like the one she'd experienced?

"Are you getting your book signed?" At Tammie's question Erin noticed that people were queued up, holding their books.

"Yes, I am," Erin stood. "I must admit to being a bit surprised at the direction of this story. I've read many of her books. Fantasy romance is one of my favorite genres."

Tammie giggled. "And I can't help but wonder if you are meant to be here."

Letting out a sigh, Erin gave her new friend what she thought to be a wry look. "I knew you were going to say that."

Moments later, Erin approached the author who gave her a warm look. "There is something compelling about you," the woman said pointedly, looking into Erin's eyes.

"In one of your interviews, you were acclaimed as a prolific medium. Is that true?" Erin asked as Tammie, Sabrina, and Gwen moved closer with curious expressions.

Daniella shrugged. "I consider myself more of a foreteller. I can sometimes see things that will affect people. I am rarely wrong." Her lips curved as she scanned Erin's face.

"You are keeping a secret. Very soon, you will have to face not only your fears but also an experience that will forever change the course of your life." Daniella blinked as if coming out of a trance and busied herself opening the book.

"That sounds a bit ominous," Erin said, her voice steady despite the thudding of her heart.

"Not at all," Daniella responded, as she signed the book with a flourish. "Stay the course and all will be well."

When she turned away to take one of the sisters' books, Erin walked to the table where the food and beverages were and poured herself a glass of champagne that had been opened as soon as the reading ended. She drained the glass and refilled it.

Tammie neared and filled a flute with the bubbly liquid. "That was interesting."

"Before you ask me. I am still not convinced, but I will consider helping you. I am in the process of moving, so next week is the soonest I can come to Dunimarle," Erin said, referring to the castle. "I am not sure why I am doing this."

"Oh my goodness," Tammie whispered and put the glass down. Then with her usual exuberance, she clapped softly and bounced on her toes. "I am so happy. We have to get Padraig out."

Not wanting to have to speak to the author again and hear another foreboding message, Erin walked to the front of the shop, said her farewells, and hurried out. The jarring difference between the interior of the bookstore and the outside was stark. The air was chilly, autumn soon turning into winter.

It was Erin's first night in her new flat. She wandered from one room to the other, a bright smile on her face. Her new home was bright and spacious, almost double the size of her last place.

She didn't dare question her good fortune, curious as it was that she was able to claim it before anyone else. Moving to the French doors, she longed for spring to start planting out in the small enclosed garden. Already she'd found several nurseries where she could buy indoor plants that would thrive from all the light.

Her mind went back to the day before, the words Daniella McFadden had read and how she'd somehow caused Erin to rashly agree to help Tammie. She'd gotten caught up in the moment. What Daniella had stated was vague and could have been said to anyone causing the person to interpret it in a way that was personal.

Turning away from the view, she lowered to the couch and stared blankly at her cell phone. She should cancel, make up an excuse. Letting out a sigh, she brought up Tammie's phone number and her thumb hovered over the send button.

"Do you live here?"

The masculine voice made Erin jump to her feet and shriek at the same time. Later she'd ponder her immediate reaction of throwing her phone at the intruder leaving her without an option of calling for help.

Padriag Clarre stood in the middle of the room, looking as if he belonged there. "When did you move in?"

"Wh-what the hell are you doing in my flat?" Erin stalked to the French doors and threw them open. "Get out of my house." She pointed to the open doors.

Instead of making to leave, he frowned at her. "Technically, this is my home."

Dressed in a manner that could only be described as a casual mixture of medieval and modern, somehow he pulled it off. The tunic top over jeans and leather boots under a thick fur coat was definitely an interesting combination.

"This is not your home. How did you get in?" Erin glared at him, her arm still outstretched toward the open doorway.

His wide shoulders lifted and lowered, his expression bland. "Do you really need to ask? I materialized from the other realm. Where you were awed by my incredible masculinity and sword fighting."

It was Erin's turn to return the bland stare. "You were not that impressive."

"Ha! So you admit it. You were in awe."

She took a tentative step toward him, meeting the hazel gaze with her own. "Did it really happen? Are you really trapped there?"

There was a flicker of something, the carefully held mask slipping for an instant, and she recognized fear and perhaps sadness. Before she could be sure which, his expression of nonchalance returned.

"Some say trapped, others called it an adventure."

"It is not an adventure if you can't leave at your own will."

Padriag walked to the French doors, his gaze on the garden. His closeness gave Erin the opportunity to study him closer. Tall, about six feet, with reddish hair that brushed his shoulders and a mustache and a closely cropped beard of the same red hue, he looked to be more Irish than Scottish. Scanning his body, hesitating on his butt, she had to admit the man was built perfectly.

When he glanced at her, she felt her cheeks warm. "So answer my questions," she said, hoping he didn't notice her pinkened cheeks or quickened pulse.

"It did happen, although you missed the best part. You were passed out when the dragon swept us away from Meliot's castle." He let out a breath and nodded. "And aye, I am not free to leave."

"I remember parts of it." Erin went on. "Why have the others been able to escape and not you?"

This time he seemed reluctant to answer. "Do you have any Irn-Bru? I'm thirsty," he said, referring to the popular Scottish soft drink and obviously avoiding answering her question.

"I do," Erin said, walking to her newly stocked refrigerator. "The only reason is because my cousin, Aubrey, loves it. I don't drink it myself, its nothing but sugar." She took the bottle out and held it out for Padriag. "I don't think sweet carbonated beverages are healthy for you."

"Being that I'm about three hundred years old, I don't worry too much about what's good and bad for me."

Taking the proffered beverage, Padriag's other hand closed over hers, his gaze locking with hers. A ripple of awareness traveled down her body.

"Do not feel obligated to help me, Erin. I understand your hesitation. If it is my fate to remain behind, there must be a reason for it."

Erin had to drag her eyes away. Whatever she wished to believe, there was no denying the fact that she was not only compelled to save him, but damn if she wasn't more attracted to this man than any other she'd ever met. She lifted her hand to reach out and touch his face, stopping halfway and snatching it down. What the hell was wrong with her?

"I do wish to help, it is just that, I don't have the gift, like Tammie and the others. Honestly, I am not sure how I can possibly be of any assistance. What if ..." her voice trailed, unsure of what she wanted to say. What if she made things worse?

When his gaze fell to her lips, Erin's breath caught. Was he going to kiss her? Why did she want him to?

"I am content to think on the 'what ifs' with you." Padriag replied, his voice taking on a husky tone. "Take your time, if it is meant to happen it will. If not, then again, there is a reason for it."

Lowering her gaze, Erin inhaled. "I ..." The hold on her hand lessened.

He was gone.

"I will help," she said to the empty room.

Chapter Four

A deafening, bone-rattling pounding slammed against the thick wooden and iron-clad door of the keep, each impact reverberating through the solid stone walls. Everything inside seemed to tremble with the force of the assault. Outside, guttural howls and piercing roars filled the night, a chilling cacophony of Meliot's wolf sentinels rallying, anxious to come inside and do what they did best, tear into flesh with their razor-like fangs. The unholy army was ready. Ready to destroy anything or anyone in their path the moment the doors gave way.

"Get down!" Liam's voice cut through the chaos an instant before an arrow shrieked past Padraig's ear, so close he felt the unnatural heat of its flight. It struck with a violent thud into the wooden beam at the center of the keep's great hall, quivering like a living thing.

Through the narrow slits of the windows, shadows moved with unsettling speed—Meliot's archers. Their forms grotesque combinations of human torsos fused onto the bodies of beasts, their muscular flanks shifting with unnatural grace. They were fabled for their deadly accuracy, and somehow, impossibly, their arrows found paths through even the smallest openings.

Another arrow flew through the air. This time, Padraig wasn't so lucky. An arrow raked his arm, slicing deep. Hot pain exploded. He hissed between his teeth, clutching the wound as warm blood seeped between his fingers.

"I told you to get down," Liam barked, his tone sharp with exasperation. He flattened himself against the wall next to a narrow archer's slot cut into the stones, his bowstring taut. Then, with a single, fluid motion, he slid sideways, loosed an arrow, and ducked back just as quickly. "Got one right between the eyes," he announced, smug satisfaction in his tone.

Padraig cursed under his breath, tore a strip from the bottom of his tunic and bound the wound hastily, using his teeth to tighten the knot. "I hope you killed the bastard who got me."

Another violent impact rocked the door. This time, the force sent dust sifting down from the rafters. Still, the iron-reinforced wood held, unyielding. Tristan, with the power of superhuman strength, and craftsman Niall, had crafted these defenses to withstand an army. Every hinge, every iron bar across the entry had been forged with a singular purpose —to keep monsters like Meliot's forces out. But for how long?

Then, something shifted. A low, unnatural hum buzzed through the air, the kind that made a man's bones feel brittle, the hairs on his arms prickle.

"My wards are completely gone," Padraig muttered, a sick realization tightening his gut.

He pushed to his feet, snatching up his bow, ignoring the sharp pull in his wounded arm. Pressing his back against the wall, he braced himself before twisting and letting loose an arrow. It found its mark—a centaur-like beast snarled in agony as the shaft buried deep in its midsection before it crumpled.

But there were more. Too many.

Blowing out a breath, he turned to Liam. "There are at least fifty archers out there. We can't keep this up."

"Try the wards again!" Liam ducked as another arrow screamed past, embedding itself into the stone wall with a crack. He turned, eyes wide. "That one nearly took my head off."

A sudden, earth-shaking impact sent them both stumbling. The walls shuddered violently, a rain of dust and splinters cascading from the rafters.

"What the hell was that?" Padraig dropped low, then risked a glance through the window. His blood ran cold.

"A bloody catapult," he breathed, unable to suppress a flicker of awe—before dread overtook it. "That's ... actually kind of impressive."

"Not when it's being used to reduce our keep to rubble!" Liam snapped. "The wards, Padraig! Now!"

Gritting his teeth, Padraig threw his hands up, and magic surged from his fingertips in a searing blue light, crackling like raw energy. He focused everything into fortifying the invisible barrier that surrounded them, but something was wrong. The power of the wards that had held strong for centuries was growing weaker. The dark magic pressing against them had changed—grown stronger, either that or his power was diminishing.

Sweat beaded along his temple. His breathing hitched as exhaustion threatened to drag him under. He was fighting against something vast, something relentless.

And he was losing.

Finally, the wards reformed, those at the door flew backward, the dark army stopped shooting arrows when they bounced back, injuring several. Padriag's breath rasped in and out of his lungs, sweat trickling down his face.

Through the windows, both Liam and Padriag followed the enemies' movements as they retreated and disappeared into the forest.

"How's the arm?" Liam asked, his bright blue gaze locked on the crudely tied bandage.

"I'll live," Padriag replied, flinching. "I don't know what they put on their arrowheads, but my skin is still burning."

After boiling herbs and adding a splash of whiskey, Liam helped clean the wound. Then they sat in front of the fireplace contemplating what had occurred.

"You are aware that you cannot stay here alone," Liam said. "They will return, over and over."

Padriag drank the rest of the whiskey in his cup and poured another serving. "If I am to be the one left here, I want to live here, in our home. Besides, I have no idea how we'd get to Esland without our horses. Even then, do we know where exactly it is?"

His friend shrugged. "I am sure we'll eventually find our way to Esland." He pondered further. "Meliot thinks there are two of us left. Still furious about the others being rescued, he probably wants to take us prisoner so we cannot escape."

What his friend said was what he'd been thinking. "Promise me that if they ever do get through, you will immediately dematerialize and return to Scotland. I want a vow from you that you will go." Padriag met Liam's eyes. "Promise me."

Liam looked away, his gaze on the fire. "I will not leave you at his mercy. I am no fool, I will disappear, but I will return to rescue you. Know that. All I will vow is to leave, but only so that I can return and help you."

"I guess that will have to do," Padriag replied. "This is nice whiskey. I think we should open another bottle and get totally and absolutely pissed."

"Sounds like a great idea." Liam stood. "I'll get it."

FOR OVER A WEEK, there had been no sign of Meliot's dark forces. Despite it, when Liam left to go to Scotland, Padriag fortified his wards and remained inside, ensuring every window shutter stayed closed and bolted.

One morning just after Liam had returned the night before, loud knocks on the front door startled Padriag awake. He'd been sitting in front of the fireplace contemplating how to get to the land where Prince Sterling ruled and must have fallen asleep.

By the time he stood, Liam came down the stairs and headed for the door.

"Wait!" Padriag called out. "We don't just open doors

here. We do not have friendly neighbors coming over to borrow a cup of sugar. Our neighbors are assholes that want to eat us."

Liam gave him a droll look. "I foresaw this visitor. He is safe." With that, he removed the crossbar and opened the door to a tall, muscular man dressed in leathers.

The pale skinned, silver-haired visitor had the bearing and build of a warrior. Ice-blue eyes moved from Liam to Padriag. "I am called Veylen, I am here to escort you to Esland."

"How are we to travel?" Padriag asked. "I didn't hear the dragon."

"Mounts await for us in the forest. I assume you can dematerialize from here." Not waiting for a reply, Veylen turned back to the door. "We must go at once, the veil you've cast that is keeping your enemies away will not last much longer."

"That's rude," Padriag said. "My wards are pretty strong."

Veylen turned to look at him. "Then how did I get to your doorway?"

Padriag narrowed his eyes, to see the woven pattern of his magical barrier. It looked to be intact except for an opening directly in front of the door. "Good question."

It didn't take long for Liam and Padriag to strap on daggers and swords and grab the sacks they'd already packed. As one the three of them dematerialized following Veylen's trail until materializing in a forest.

"What in the four-legged hell are those?" Padriag pointed

at enormous saddled beasts, unable to keep his mouth from falling open.

The strange animals pawed at the earth, their colossal hooves striking the ground with a deep, resonant thud. Their hulking bodies of thick, dark gray hide were twice the size of a Clydesdale yet bore the unmistakable power and bulk of a bull rather than the sleek frame of a horse. Towering antlers arched skyward, their points razor-sharp, elongated snouts with tusks gave them a fierce, boar-like visage. A strange, iridescent sheen glazed their eyes—a trait that, perhaps, allowed them to see in darkness.

"Aurochs," Veylen snapped, his impatience evident as he seized the reins and hoisted himself onto the back of one of the creatures. "Mount, we must hurry."

Padriag and Liam exchanged brief glances before following suit, slinging their sacks onto the wide saddles before climbing up. The moment Padriag settled atop the beast, he felt an unexpected sense of security. The sheer height, the immense power beneath him was unlike riding any horse.

As they surged forward, the aurochs galloped with a breathtaking blend of power and grace, their massive frames defying expectation. Their long, muscular strides devoured the rugged terrain with effortless precision, hooves striking the earth in a steady, rhythmic cadence. Despite their imposing size, their movements were remarkably fluid, each motion rolling seamlessly into the next, as if the land itself bowed beneath their weight. Perched atop the broad back, Padriag felt little more than a smooth, swaying motion—no harsh jolts or bone-rattling shocks, only the sensation of gliding forward with an unstoppable force.

After about half a day of travel they arrived at the edge of Atlandia. to a land neither Liam nor Padriag had ever been. It was Sterling's realm, which, according to rumors they'd heard, was a forbidden place for anyone not from there.

It struck Padriag as strange, since Sterling was brother to the rulers of Atlandia. But then again, sibling rivalry and all that. Perhaps in the past there had been some sort of disagreement between them bringing about the set boundaries.

Veylen looked over to them, brows lowered, and lips pressed together in a stern way. It was as if he was unsure they were worthy of entering his homeland.

"We are entering Esland, once in our realm, departing is against our laws," he called out.

Liam and Padriag exchanged droll looks. "Dramatic," Padriag murmured under his breath. Obviously Veylen heard it because he turned and glared at him.

They crossed through what looked to be a thick mist that made it impossible to see anything past their noses. Obviously, the aurochs were unaffected as they continued forward at the same fast speed.

Slowly, mists dissipated as aurochs continued forward, but at a slower pace, giving Padriag an opportunity to observe the startling new surroundings. This was a land like nothing he could even imagine.

Plush hills and valleys covered in lush vegetation resembling moss, as far as the eye could see. Trees of every size reached toward the vibrant yellow skies that reminded him of sunset although the suns were still high, partly hiding behind effervescent pinkish clouds. On several hillsides, a sort of drizzle fell, that caused a myriad of rainbows. Colorful bird-like creatures with long tails soared from the treetops, through the rainbows circling, wings outstretched.

The vast valley was split by a road on which they traveled, that was flanked on both sides by deep ravines with no visible bottom. Padriag ensured a strong hold on the reins and leaned to the right to peer over the edge. Other than trees and moss, he couldn't see how deep the chasm was.

"Falling would suck," he murmured. Liam glanced over to him with a look of agreement and motioned to the hillside with his eyes.

Spaced out on both sides of the ravine, men with long hair and muscular builds watched them from astride more aurochs. By the wicked, wide-bladed weapons strapped to their backs, it was obvious they were warriors. Probably part of Sterling's army. Every kingdom needed an army, and in Padriag's opinion, he doubted any enemies would make it far into this one.

Moments later, the symphony of cascading water swallowed the lilting calls of the birds. As they crested a towering hill, its slopes thick with moss-laden trees, a breathtaking sight unfurled before them. Rising from the cliffside like ancient sentinels stood a collection of castle-like structures. The sand-hued stone walls should have been a stark contrast to the beautiful landscape, and yet, with tangles of vines growing down the sides, they melded into the surroundings.

Beneath the structures, waterfalls, luminous in the sunlight, tumbled from the heights, spilling over the rocky ledges and plunging into the vast lake below. Mist curled from the churning waters, weaving an ethereal veil around the majestic strongholds. It was as if the very air whispered of the beautiful surroundings.

"Wow," Padriag said, looking at Liam, who seemed as awestruck as he was. "I won't be surprised if dancing plates and forks greet us inside."

Veylen frowned at Padriag, obviously not understanding what he implied.

Mounted guards patrolled across the entrance to a bridge over the water, another set at the gates. "The bridge to the village is heavily guarded. Never attempt to leave on your own. You will not make it across it alive."

"That's welcoming," Liam said, his tone dry.

"If that's a village, what does the actual castle look like?" Padriag muttered under his breath.

Genuinely curious, he scratched his head. "What is the harm in us wishing to explore out here?"

There was silence for a few minutes before Veylen replied. "Our people rarely travel outside the villages. Most of the vegetation is poisonous or carnivorous. Deadly predators roam freely. Only our warriors or citizens who are expertly trained, are safe outside the walls."

"You convinced me," Padriag stated. "Inside the village it is."

Liam wasn't as trusting. "These beasts seem at ease while traversing the land. Why is that?"

"They are native to Esland. Impervious to the poison plants and because of their speed and size, only one predator would be bold enough to attack them."

Silence followed until Padriag couldn't take it. "Okay, I'll bite. What predator is that?"

When Veylen slid a look in his direction, he could swear there was a twinkle of humor in his eyes. "Dragons of course."

"Duh," Padriag said, slapping the side of his head.

"So there are other dragons here besides Sterling's?" Liam asked, looking up to the sky.

"Aye, there are more." Veylen's answer was vague, perhaps the number of dragons in Esland was a secret.

ONCE THEY CROSSED THE BRIDGE, they entered what Veylen called the villages. Paved roads flanked by stairs crisscrossed endlessly, leading to different doorways. They continued past a marketplace, lines of tents under which people sold wares and what looked to be public buildings, like shops and gathering halls. A short distance away, Padriag noticed what looked to be a recreational area, where people strolled about.

The villagers, both men and women were all of a pale complexion with silver hair. All wore long, tunic style clothes that stopped just above the ankles. The women seemed to favor more colorful fabrics accentuated with beaded necklaces and bracelets. The men wore muted colored tunics, sandals, and round boxy hats.

Whenever they passed, the people stopped and stared at them with open curiosity. Some greeted Veylen warmly, others seemed more reserved, only bowing their heads in acknowledgement.

Finally, they came to a broad road where he spotted what had to be the castle, since there were huge guards mounted on aurochs flanking the gates.

Groups of people moved along the sides of the road walking to and from the large structure. Others drove ladened carts pulled by creatures resembling mules, except for lack of ears and shorter snouts.

Surprisingly, although majestic with its flag-topped turrets and guards, the castle was not unlike the other buildings in the city.

The aurochs their party had ridden from their distant keep seemed to be anticipating a meal and rest. They picked up speed and within a pair of minutes they passed through a set of massive open gates.

Inside the castle walls, there was activity, people milling about and guards patrolling in pairs.

Without prodding the well-trained aurochs stopped in front of a doorway and lowered to their knees making it easy for the riders to dismount.

Padriag untied his sack of belongings and jumped down, landing softly on booted feet as Liam did the same.

Standing in the doorway, Sterling motioned for them to join him, and they went up the steps and into the cool interior of the castle.

Just then two women, one with the same coloring as Veylen and Sterling—pale skin, almost luminescent and silver hair—neared and took their sacks. Sterling said something to them in a language Padriag had not heard before. The women stole glances toward him and Liam before hurrying away.

"They will prepare your chambers and ensure you have anything needed to make your stay comfortable," the prince informed them.

"Come inside, tell me what is happening in the other realms." He walked to a table and sank into a comfortable chair.

They told Sterling about the attacks at the keep and Padriag revealed that it was becoming harder to travel between the worlds. At speaking the words out loud, a lump seemed to lodge in his throat. He covered it up by clearing it, hoping the men didn't notice.

Admittedly, Esland was beautiful, but it wasn't where he expected to live out the rest of his life. At the end of three hundred years from the day they'd been thrown into this alter-world, he would become mortal and begin aging at a normal human rate until finally dying. And that deadline was soon approaching.

After such a long life, Padriag welcomed the idea of becoming mortal. And yet, it hurt to think that he would never set his eyes on his friends again, not touch his native Scotland, breath the mossy air, see the craggy mountains overgrown with heather. A vise tightened around his chest making it impossible to breathe. He bent at the waist, his mouth opening and closing like a fish out of water.

Something gripped his shoulders, pulling him upward to stand straight. "Padriag," Liam calm voice broke through panic that overtook as he felt himself begin to lose the fight to live. Why was air refusing to enter his body? Desperate, Padriag gripped Liam's tunic.

"You can breathe, draw it in, slowly." Liam inhaled deeply making Padriag want to punch him.

"Ah-ah, I-I c-cannot," he gasped as the edges of his vision blurred. "H-help m-me."

"You can. Do it now slowly ... inhale, blow it out."

Lungs screamed for air until it finally flowed into him, and he gulped in a breath and then another. He collapsed against Liam, embarrassed over what had occurred in Sterling's presence. It was the first time he'd ever had such a reaction.

"Panic attack." Sterling expression remained stoic, emotionless as always. "Perhaps you would prefer to rest in your bedchamber. Someone will come fetch you at mealtime."

"I'd prefer a walk to clear my head," Padriag said, pushing away from Liam, his legs still not quite steady.

His breathing was harsh, but thankfully the pounding heartbeats were slowing. Without looking at either man, he stalked from the room before realizing he had no idea if there were any private gardens or such.

A skinny young boy of about ten, came up to him and smiled. He said something in the strange language motioning for him to follow. Once outside, the lanky boy hurried away from the courtyard calling out something to other children who looked to Padriag and then to the boy with admiration. Obviously, the job of guiding the newcomer was a position of honor.

They arrived at a path and the boy pointed to it, then made walking motions with his hand and led Padriag to a walking path.

Padriag bowed his head in gratitude as he'd seen others do and the boy's face brightened, a wide grin stretching across his face before turning and running off.

The pathway led into a labyrinth of sorts, winding between purple trimmed hedges and flowering bushes of a lavender hue. Here and there benches were scattered, but he didn't see another soul whilst making his way through. There was no clear path, but because the hedges were only about five feet tall, he could easily spot the castle and figure out which direction to head when he was ready to leave.

"Shit. Shit. Shit," he repeated. His mind whirled. He lowered himself to a bench, bending forward and holding his head. This was not at all what the rest of his life was supposed to be. If he lived to be eighty, he would be here for almost sixty years.

Rumbling roars sounded in the distance and Padriag searched the empty sky. Moments later the unmistakable whomp, whomp, whomp of huge wings vibrated from above. Moments later, the roars, like those of angry lions or elephants, accompanied the sound of wings as they became louder. Four huge dragons flew into view, their colossal bodies inspiring awe and fear as they continued calling out, perhaps communicating with each other. The beasts were beautiful, of different coloring, some a luminescent green, others light hues of blues and purples. The sunlight seemed to reflect off of them while they flew in circles as if patrolling the land below.

Padriag watched them, his gloom forgotten for the moment, becoming lost in the unbelievable magnificence of the creatures flying above.

Chapter Five

Fog swirled around her ankles, rising inch by inch until fully encircling her. A low gravelly voice she couldn't quite place repeated the same words over and over. "Come to me. Come to me."

There was a parting of sorts, the fog moving away as she walked forward, her footfalls silenced by the mossy undergrowth. Vines seemed to reach out to her, wrapping around her arms gently, as if caressing her skin.

The urge to escape, to get away, became stronger as the voice became louder, closer. Tears streaked down her cheeks. She had to get away, had to run, but her legs were so heavy, her movements labored until she was frozen in place. Looking down, she realized the vines had wrapped tightly around her legs, waist, and shoulders, holding her in place.

With a woosh, the mist evaporated and a man in robes appeared in the distance, long straight gray hair down his back, black malevolent eyes and mouth twisted into a gleeful smile. "You are mine."

Erin fought against the vines, screaming in terror.

Mouth dry, breathing harsh, Erin bolted upright to sit, relief pouring over her at realizing she was in her bed, in her bedroom. She was safe.

The old man in the dream was familiar. Erin knew his name and where he lived. Meliot, the wizard, the evil man who'd trapped Padriag. Unless she did something, he was going to come for her, there was no doubt in her mind. There was no choice in the matter, it was time.

Reaching for her phone, she found the number and pressed call.

"Hi John. Can we talk?"

THE NEXT DAY she went to Stewart's Books & Magic and spent hours talking with John. According to John, his partner Liam, a handsome blond knight, was the only one of the four men who'd been rescued that could continue to travel between the realms. And he could ferry messages between the worlds.

Despite Erin's disbelief she'd be useful in Padriag's rescue, John insisted that she'd been chosen by fate. If nothing else, she had to do it to save herself.

DUNIMARLE CASTLE WAS BEAUTIFUL, but not ostentatious, a subtle beauty of gray stone, surrounded by expansive lands. She drove down a cobbled one lane road that curved at the front arched doorway. Several cars were parked to the left side of the castle under modern built covered stalls. A golf cart had been driven to the front and left, probably by someone working around the lands.

Erin drove to the parking stalls and pulled into an empty one, then sat in the car for a few moments collecting her thoughts.

Once she reached the front door of the castle, it was opened by Tammie, her eyes sparkling as they met Erin's. "I am so happy to see you, friend." The American opened her arms inviting a hug. Erin had to smile as she leaned forward allowing the closeness.

"There is much to do," Tammie said, motioning for her to enter. "We are all in the library," Tammie continued as she led Erin toward a doorway.

Her breath caught as she walked into the room. Inside were Tammie's sisters, Gwen and Sabrina, as well as three astonishingly handsome men, Tristan McRainey, laird of the castle, Gavin Campbell and Niall MacTavish, who'd been trapped in the other realm until recently. The trio, along with Liam, were all rescued by their current loves.

Was she to be relegated to being Padriag's lover if she rescued him? Was that part of the bargain? Not that it would be a horrible fate, given the man was drop-dead gorgeous, but love had to be involved before she would ever commit to any man, and although attracted, she was doubtful it would happen.

Also, she doubted the current strange situation would lead to it.

"Hello Erin, we are so glad you are here," Gwen, the eldest sister said, giving her a warm smile. She slid a look to the trio of men and then back to her. "I hope they don't intimidate you. I insisted they be here to answer any questions you may have about the alter-world."

Hearing footsteps behind, she turned to see John hurry in, his glasses slightly askew, a pile of books in his arms. Despite being disheveled, the man remained curiously attractive. "So sorry, I lost track of time." He walked past her to drop the books on a large round table. "Have you started?"

"Not yet," Tammie chimed. "Erin just arrived." She motioned toward the various chairs surrounding the table. "Sit down, everyone."

"Wine?" Gwen asked, already pouring a glass of red.

"Yes, please," Erin replied, needing something to help her get through whatever came next. The glass was pushed into her hand, and she drank the bittersweet liquid as she settled into one of the chairs at the table.

Tristan met her gaze for a moment. "As you are aware, each of us have required someone in this realm to assist in our release from the entrapment. Meliot, the wizard you encountered, has been quite adept at making our escapes difficult."

"Although his power seemed to be diminishing as of late, we cannot underestimate his capabilities," Gavin interjected. "He is furious at our escape and is making it almost impossible for Padriag."

Erin's chest tightened. Padriag hadn't said anything about what occurred in the other realm when he'd appeared at her flat. "Is Padriag in danger?"

"He will have to relocate," Gwen informed her. "Liam informed us that Sterling, who reigns over a different realm called Esland, has offered Padriag asylum. We have not heard from either in a few days, hopefully it is because they have gone to Esland."

They waited, every pair of eyes on her for the information to percolate. A myriad of questions whirled in her head. "Will he be able to travel here from there?"

"I am not sure." It was Gavin who spoke again. "We believe so, but will wait to hear from Liam, who should be returning in a day or two at the most."

John's stricken expression revealed that he'd not been aware of what had been transpiring. "Why was I not told about this?" The tension in his voice brought everyone to exchange looks.

"I'm so sorry John," Tammie said. "I thought Liam had told you."

"I wasn't aware of this *Sterling's* invitation." His emphasis on the prince's name made Erin think that perhaps there was jealousy behind it.

"Sterling was not forthcoming with information about timing. We are speculating it has happened, we are not sure," Tristan explained, his tone flat. It was obvious the man was used to leadership and not prone to sentimentalism.

Erin slid a look to Gwen who gave Tristan a pointed look before speaking. "I assure you John, Liam is not being deceitful. He honestly didn't know when it would happen."

Considering John's tight lips, he wasn't happy. He pushed books out to the three sisters and Erin. "I brought some of the books that pulled at me. For the last few days I've been evoking help from the goddesses to help us."

"Do you have any questions for us?" Niall asked, his dark

eyes meeting hers. "There is naught we won't do to free Padriag."

"What were the strategies needed to free each of you?" Erin pulled a pen pouch and notebook from her tote and proceeded to carefully choose a pen. Opening the notebook, she held the pen at the ready.

Tristan counted off with his fingers, starting with his thumb. "A spell, contact with our intended rescuer, the deciphering of our curse ..." he stopped and looked to Gwen.

"Each specific curse seems to require actions to be taken by the rescuer. It is hard to explain," Gwen added. "It was different for each of us. Not just figuring out how to break the curse but also maneuvering around Meliot and other factors."

Erin was aware that Niall had not only been imprisoned by Meliot in the alter-world, but also a demon called Devina had kept him ensnared in a separate trap, holding him hostage when he slept.

"Are any of you aware if there are other holds on Padriag?"

Gavin nodded. "I think something, perhaps Meliot, is interfering with his ability to move between the realms. He told us it was becoming difficult for him to do so."

Why had Padriag not said any of this to her? Erin scribbled down the information, holding the pen tightly.

"Does something bother you?" Gwen asked.

Erin let out a long breath. "Padriag came to my flat, a couple days ago. He was confused that I was there." Tension filled the room as she continued.

"It turns out that I just moved into his ancestral home."

Speaking the words out loud brought the realization of what a huge "coincidence" it was that she'd been compelled to move into that particular home.

"How long was he there?" Niall asked leaning forward, his expression strained.

"Not very long, just minutes."

This time Gavin spoke, his deep voice as enthralling as his face. "What did he say? Did he ask for anything?"

Erin closed her eyes for a moment. "He didn't actually say much. Seemed resigned to remain behind. He told me not to feel obligated to help him, that he was last for a reason, although I got the impression he doesn't understand why."

Everyone sat in silence, contemplating.

"This is part of his curse," Tammie said, breaking the silence and giving a pointed look to her notebook.

Three lives rescued
Three moons high
Two hearts restored
One must die

"That's kind of ominous," Erin stared at the words on her paper.

Tammie shook her head. "The strange thing is that this all happened already. When the three moons were out, Niall and I got together, he along with you and I were rescued and Davina died."

"We think there is another part to the curse and have to find out what it is. Padriag may not remember it, or perhaps it is hidden." Gwen's words were tinged with frustration.

"That could be why it has been too hard to rescue Padriag," John said. "Without knowing what binds him, it is almost impossible to come up with a spell."

What they said made sense. Erin felt useless, the least qualified to help in the matter. She let out a long sigh. "I've been having strange dreams since ... I returned from the alter-world."

As she told them about the mists and the creepy plants that caught her, everyone listened intently. John scribbled notes furiously, peppering her with questions about each single detail. Things she'd not thought about became clearer.

"There were moons in the sky, but I don't remember how many. The mists moved up and down. The vines were a strange color, not green, but more a deep purple." Erin was shocked at how many details she remembered.

Was it possible that the hints to breaking the spell had been with her all along? The dreams, although scary, always ended exactly before anything could hurt her.

"Next time you dream, be sure to write down any details you notice right away," Gwen told her. "I know it's hard to want to relive a nightmare, but it could be the only way to help him. You are dreaming for a reason."

"We need to get started," Sabrina stated, giving her husband, Gavin, a pointed look. As the trio of men stood, each gave Erin looks of expectation. It was terrible that they hung their hopes on her. She wasn't ready for such a great responsibility. Every one of her senses screamed for her to explain it was all a colossal mistake and run from the room, get in her car and drive until she was out of Scotland.

Sabrina pushed back from the table walked to the

doorway and closed the door. Gwen lit candles around the room that Erin had not noticed until then. Tammie turned off the lights while John cleared the table of the books he'd brought. Obviously the four had worked together before as each tended to a task without speaking.

Finally, they all sat at the table, and Erin looked from one to the other waiting for whatever came next.

John squeezed her right hand. "We will seek help from the spirit world. Your job is to be the vessel. What I need you to do is to close your eyes and keep them closed the entire time." Erin did as he instructed. "Let out a breath and inhale. Let it out, inhale."

At the soft sound of his urgings, Erin felt fear and stress melt away.

"Now I want you to picture a huge box, large enough for you to fit in. Do you see it?"

Erin nodded, picturing a large white box with a side entrance.

"Get inside and make yourself comfortable," John continued. "Now I need you to hear this and believe it." He hesitated, giving her time to settle and take a few more breaths.

"Nothing can enter this box to harm you. If anything enters, it is to help, give comfort and reassurance. Only good things can come into the box. Understand?"

Again Erin nodded.

"Empty your mind," Gwen said in a soft tone. "Concentrate on the warmth inside the box, let our words flow around you. You do not have to understand or hear them.

Your work is to receive whatever comes to you from other sources."

Erin sensed warmth and was comfortable inside the imaginary box. Strangely the box gave her a safe place to be, and she didn't mind being there.

The four others began reciting.

"Everlasting Beings of power,
Spirits of Light
Come forth to this place
Give us the Sight."

The chants lulled Erin into a sleepy state, soon the words of their continuous chanting blurred into something akin to a melody.

Lights flickered and Erin considered they were the product of her eyes being closed. It was normal to see specks of light. But these were different, they were like fairies flying in circular patterns. First a couple, then joined by another pair. Whatever they were, they were fast as she couldn't make out their shapes.

A brighter light appeared in the center of her sight, it was a blueish hue, seeming to move closer. Erin tensed, but when John squeezed her hand, she remembered that only good things could enter the safety of the box.

The light floated, beautiful blue lights swirling around and through it. Whatever it was glowed brighter and then dimmer until forming a humanlike form.

She couldn't make out the being's features, but whatever it was wore long, white, flowing robes with golden edging.

Words appeared in her mind, swirling in space, as if floating. She could both see and hear them.

Until moon's pale light and dawn's last breath,
I send thee to the brink of death.
Chains of darkness, will not unbind—
Never to be released, your soul, or your mind.

"Open your eyes," John's voice shook her back to reality, and she happily obeyed. Despite the dimness of the room, she had to blink several times before able to see clearly.

"I know what the curse is," she said in a hoarse whisper. "It's pretty bad."

Chapter Six

Aubrey wore black leggings that hugged her well-toned frame, paired effortlessly with a bright yellow tank top—a bold color that glowed against her rich skin, the kind of shade only a deeper complexion could truly pull off. Despite the eye-catching hue, the outfit maintained an easy, casual vibe, like she hadn't even tried ... and still nailed it.

Erin had just finished explaining everything and waited for her cousin's reaction.

"Oh. My. God." Aubrey sat cross-legged on the couch, a bottle of Irn-Bru halfway to her gaped mouth. "Are you serious?" Her wide brown eyes were pinned to Erin as if she expected her to suddenly disappear.

"Why haven't you told me any of this before?" Her cousin placed the soft drink on the side table and jumped to her feet.

Her cousin began walking around the room. If pacing while stressed was an Olympic sport, Aubrey would be a gold medalist. "Another realm? Knights? Men stuck? Enchantments."

Erin sat back allowing her cousin to digest everything she'd just dumped on her. She'd needed someone to confide in, and her cousin and she had been best friends practically since birth.

"I know it's a lot. I wanted to be sure I wasn't crazy before telling you anything. Although, saying it all out loud doesn't make me sound sane, if I'm honest," Erin mused. "Quite the opposite."

"What do you need me to do? I want to help," Aubrey stopped pacing to look at her. "What's next?"

"Wait for the dream, I guess."

"What is the spell again?" Aubrey asked.

"We refer to it as the curse. The spell is what I have to come up with to save him," Erin clarified, feeling a bit out of sorts to be having the conversation in the first place.

She repeated the curse from the notes in her notebook, despite the fact she'd repeated it so many times on the drive home she probably knew it by heart.

"Aubrey, can you stay here for a couple nights? Just in case the dream comes and it's different. I'm a bit shaken and could use company." Rubbing both hands down her face she blew out a breath. "I'm probably being paranoid."

Aubrey plopped down next to her. "I would be. This is all so weird. Remember when that little ghost girl used to follow us around?"

At five years old, both she and Aubrey had an imaginary friend named Lizzy. Aubrey claimed to see the little girl, and

Erin had pretended to see her as well, going along with whatever her cousin claimed to hear Lizzy say.

One day, when Erin and her mother were visiting, Aubrey squealed with delight and snatched up a newspaper that was rolled up in a basket next to the fireplace.

Erin chased after her cousin racing to where their mothers sat at the kitchen table drinking tea and chatting.

With a bright smile, Aubrey happily announced to their mothers that their little friend Lizzy was in the newspaper while pointing to the picture of a pretty blonde girl with curly hair.

Erin had been delighted as well to finally know what their imaginary friend looked like and had added. "Lizzy told us she has a brother named Henry. She doesn't like him."

"Why is Lizzy in the picture Mommy?" Aubrey had asked. It was then Erin noticed their mothers' sudden stricken looks and paled faces.

"Is Lizzy here now?" her mother had asked.

Aubrey shook her head and Erin followed suit.

Years later, Aubrey found the same newspaper page. Her mother had saved it because what they'd said was true. Lizzy's body had been found buried near a loch. She'd been dead for several years before dogs had dug up the bones. Lizzy did indeed have a brother named Henry who'd confessed to drowning his little sister accidentally when he'd been about fourteen.

"How can I ever forget it," Erin said. "Super creepy."

Aubrey chuckled. "The worst part is that the entire time I thought you saw her too. You should have been an actress."

"We were five, I'm sure my acting abilities were not that

great," Erin said with a laugh. "Let's go grab a bite. I have to go into the studio early."

THERE HADN'T BEEN any dreams the night before and Erin woke up feeling refreshed, although a bit disappointed.

Hair up in a towel, Erin pulled on her short terrycloth robe and padded into the kitchen. Aubrey had obviously left early, the note propped up next to the coffee maker letting her know she'd be back that night. She held the note wondering if Aubrey staying for a few nights would keep the dreams at bay.

If she didn't dream in the next two nights, she'd tell her cousin to stop coming. Just knowing Aubrey was there had made her feel safer. It would be hard to stay alone afterwards.

An hour later, she unlocked the door to *Namaste a While*, her pride and joy. Light scents of citrus, lavender, and vanilla from oil diffusers placed around the studio perfumed the air. Noting the light was on, Erin peeked from in front of the counter into her small office and was pleasantly surprised to find Aubrey on the laptop.

"You've always been such an early riser," Erin said, hanging her tote and jacket on hooks beside the small office doorway.

"The sunlight wakes me." Aubrey replied looking refreshed. She'd tamed her wild curls into a cute style, bunching them atop her head. Wearing the basic yoga uniform of leggings and a light sweatshirt along with soft ballet-style shoes, she looked ready for the day.

"I want to see your new routine," Aubrey continued. "I

have heard nothing but good things in our customer feedback and would like to incorporate it into my classes."

"It will be fun to have you here," Erin said. "But first before anyone arrives, I must make a cup of tea."

Aubrey frowned. "You are addicted to caffeine. Should try green tea."

"Gross," Erin replied, dunking her favorite Yorkshire black tea bag into the steaming water. "This is what keeps me going."

After adding a splash of cream, she stirred it and sipped it cautiously. "Oh, yeah baby," Erin murmured.

"You're the one that's gross," Aubrey said laughing.

"Good morning," Terra, a woman of undetermined age due to overuse of Botox, bounced in wearing a very tight neon pink ensemble. Considering how high and round her breasts were, it was obvious they were impervious to the aging process and were never, ever going to sag. "I am super excited because this is mine and George's anniversary week," Terra exclaimed. "George is taking us to the French Riviera."

"I bet that will be fun," Erin replied, contemplating why she'd never considered going there.

"After class I am shopping for bikinis," Terra boasted. "I need new tops to accommodate these babies." She clutched each breast with her hands. "Aren't they amazing?"

"We missed you," Erin said as Terra continued to hold her boobs. "Take it easy today, it's barely been six weeks since you ... er, since the new additions."

Just then, Evalyn appeared outside the shop, her rail-thin shape of sharp angles framed by the golden morning light. Of all the activities the woman did, Erin doubted there was anything Evalyn enjoyed more than smoking. Lifting a cigarette to her lips, Evalyn took a deep, deliberate drag, her red-painted nails flashing as she held it between her fingers. The ember flared, then dimmed as she exhaled a plume of smoke, watching it curl lazily in the air before she repeated the process, savoring every breath as if it were the last one in her life.

Evalyn had always been vocal about her love for smoking, especially when Erin reminded her—repeatedly—not to do it so close to the front door.

"I require shade," Evalyn had declared with a casual flick of ash toward the sidewalk. "The awning should be wider and longer, then perhaps I would stand further." Then, as though she alone possessed a secret, she whispered, "It's all those cars and birds that are harmful to humans, not cigarette smoke."

Erin waved to Evalyn to move from the door, but was promptly ignored as a petite woman, named Jane, strode up, flapping her hands dramatically to clear the smoke from her path.

"Oh, for heaven's sake, Evalyn, really?" she muttered, opening the door and scrunching her nose as she stepped inside.

Jane, a harried thirty-something mother of three, barely had time for herself, let alone patience for other's vices. She rolled her eyes and shot Erin a look as she passed. "How many times do we have to tell her to move away from the door?"

"At least there are no birds nearby," Terra quipped, in a dry tone. "Lord forbid we inhale feather dust."

Their laughter rippled behind as they moved to find the best spots to roll out their mats, the chatter light and familiar, the way it always was before class.

Outside, Evalyn lingered, drawing every possible inhalation from her cigarette, her lips pursed in satisfaction as the last wisp of smoke dissipated. Only when there was nothing left to enjoy did she finally flick the spent stub into a nearby receptacle and stride inside, trailing the scent of tobacco behind her like an expensive perfume.

Behind her, Joe Dunbar, the lone man in the early class opened the door and walked in, his gaze on the retreating Evalyn. A tall, solemn figure with an unruly mop of brown curls, Joe carried himself with the air of a professor, perpetually unimpressed.

"Good morning," he greeted the room in his usual somber tone, his voice steady. He glanced in the direction of where Evalyn had gone before turning his scrutiny to Erin. "I thought she was told not to smoke by the door."

"Good morning, Joe," Erin replied, her patience well-practiced. "I will remind her again."

"See that you do." Joe's look was pointed, the kind that made Erin feel like a student being corrected for talking during class.

Despite his grave demeanor, she liked Joe. He was a fixture of the class—a fifty-year-old confirmed bachelor, reliable as the sun, though considerably less warm.

Two additional women entered, each with a mat strapped to their backs, greeting all as they walked into the class area.

Everyone settled into their usual places. Terra and Jane

took the front row, chatting quietly. The other two women occupied the second row, Joe was in the back, his matt as far from Evalyn as possible. Near the doorway, Aubrey positioned herself slightly apart from the others, stretching idly while observing the room.

With the class poised to begin, Erin took a deep breath, shaking off the morning's minor chaos. Another day, another class, another attempt at keeping the peace.

"Namaste," Erin finished the class glancing to the back of the room as Aubrey got to her feet and smiled widely, a sign she'd enjoyed Erin's teaching.

Jane and Terra rolled their mats, making plans for coffee. "I have exactly an hour before having to pick up the girls from the school," Jane said glancing at her watch.

"Perfect," Terra confirmed. "My facial appointment is in town in two hours, just enough time for us to relax a bit more." The woman shoved the expensive mat into a matching bag, not noticing the longing and perhaps a bit of jealousy in Evalyn's expression.

After a pointed look from Erin to Evalyn, Joe then strode to exit, stopping to greet Aubrey before leaving.

Struggling to come up with a way to approach the subject of Evalyn's lack of regard for others when smoking, Erin looked on as the woman fumbled in her bag for her cigarettes.

"Evalyn, have you considered cutting back on the smoking? I worry about your health," Erin asked as the woman pulled out the pack followed by a lighter.

The woman gave her a droll look. "I have, but why deny myself the one thing I enjoy?" Evalyn coughed and tried to cover it up by clearing her throat. "I'm fit as a fiddle."

"Surely you enjoy other things," Aubrey interjected.

The woman shrugged noncommittally. "I supposed I like holding seances, and I enjoy time with my men. I do have several lovers.

Erin fought not to imagine the thin, gray-haired woman naked. It was doubtful that the woman had a number of lovers, but one never knew. "Glad to hear it."

Evalyn narrowed her eyes. "I know they complain. Obviously, no one cares of I develop a carcinoma."

"What?" Aubrey wasn't aware of Evalyn's complaint about the awning.

"The sun," Evalyn said with pointing to the ceiling. "I require shade."

The three remained silent, Erin unable to come up with anything to say.

"Maybe we can put an umbrella outside the door for you," Aubrey said with a triumphant wide smile. "You can have shade, and the others won't be subjected to cigarette smoke."

Erin braced for Evalyn's reaction. The woman stalked and leaned forward her nose a hair's breadth from Aubrey's. "And how, pray tell, am I to light my cigarette with both hands occupied. I am insulted by that suggestion."

Before Aubrey could reply, Evalyn gave a snort of satisfaction and glanced at Erin. "I will return this afternoon for Lauren's class," she informed, referring to Erin's mother.

"See you then," Erin replied with a sigh as, once again, Evalyn refused to listen to reason.

"Oh my word," Evalyn exclaimed glancing at the clock on the wall. "I best hurry or the bakery will be out of baguettes."

"I suddenly feel like a loser," Aubrey said frowning toward the doorway. "She has several lovers. I haven't had sex in almost a year."

Erin laughed. "I think I have you beat. I think she exaggerates. According to Terra, who has attended Evalyn's seances, there is usually one man, with a beak-like nose, lingering about. By the way he refers to Evalyn as "dear" he is probably the only one."

PROMPTLY AT THREE in the afternoon, the door swung open with its familiar chime, and in breezed Lauren Maguire, a whirlwind of floral fabric, gold bangles, and confidence. She paused just inside, scanning Erin with a practiced eye, her perfectly arched brow lifting.

"You should wear makeup," she announced, as if bestowing great wisdom. "You never know when Mr. Right will walk through that door." She held a hand toward the entrance, as though Prince Charming would materialize on cue.

Unlike Erin, who had barely run a brush through her hair, Lauren was immaculately styled. Her auburn locks swept into an elaborate twist, the kind that looked effortless but undoubtedly required time and skill. Her mother's sleeveless blouse, a soft coral shade, and her flowing floral skirt would have fit in better at a music festival than a yoga studio. But since her mother technically taught stretching classes, Erin had long since given up on suggesting a wardrobe change.

"Men don't grow on trees, you know," Lauren continued, launching into the same well-worn lecture. "A woman must always be presentable."

"If my future husband strolls through that door, I'll slap on some lip gloss," Erin replied, rounding the counter to press a quick kiss to her mother's cheek.

Lauren narrowed her eyes, scrutinizing Erin like a jeweler inspecting a jewel. Then her expression shifted, her lips parting in sudden revelation. "There's something different about you." Her eyes widened. "Have you met someone?"

"I have not," Erin said, a little too quickly. A man trapped in another realm probably didn't count. And even if Padraig was rescued, what were the odds some great love affair would come of it?

Before her mother could pry further, Aubrey emerged from the office, her smile bright. "Aunt Lauren! How lovely to see you."

Lauren turned, her gaze sweeping over Aubrey with the same appraising intensity. "Yes, dear, lovely to see you as well." Then, with a wag of her manicured finger, she added, "You should wear some makeup. You never know."

"Mum," Erin cut in, diverting her mother's attention. "Do you believe some people have abilities beyond explanation? Like seeing the future, casting spells ... that sort of thing?"

Lauren blinked, clearly thrown by the abrupt change in

subject. "I suppose so," she said after a pause. "I've always had a strong sense of danger when something bad will happen. Remember when I was worried about your father, and then he nearly drowned?"

Erin bit back a smile. "Mum, when he fell in the loch, he was wearing a life vest. He wasn't exactly drowning."

Lauren dismissed this with an airy wave. "He swallowed water and was very startled."

Erin shook her head, amused, but pressed on. "Does anyone in our family have 'the gift?'" She made air quotes around the words.

Her mother's gaze sharpened. "Why the sudden interest? Has something strange happened?"

"Nothing big really," Erin lied, keeping her voice casual. "I went to a book signing. The author, Daniella McFadden, claims to be a foreteller. She said something about a big change coming in my life. I wonder if it's true."

Lauren smiled knowingly. "Oh, darling, of course it's true. Everyone experiences changes. That's just how life works."

Erin let out a soft laugh, but her mother wasn't finished. "You should go to one of Evalyn's seances," she suggested. "They're quite eye-opening."

"I didn't know you went to Evalyn's," Erin said, surprised. "Who were you trying to contact?"

Her mother's expression became solemn, and Erin held her breath. "I thought your grandfather might tell me where he hid his money. I know there's cash tucked away somewhere in that rambling house of his."

Erin fought the urge to roll her eyes. "Grand is still alive, Mum. Why don't you just ask him?"

"He says he doesn't remember if he hid money or not. But as old as he is, I'm sure part of his spirit is already in the other world."

That was too much. Lauren burst into laughter, and Erin and Aubrey couldn't help but join in.

"I'm kidding," Lauren admitted between chuckles. "Honestly, I just ran out of excuses to get out of Evalyn's invitations. I was curious, so I went to see what it was about."

"And?" Aubrey prompted. "What happened?"

Lauren shrugged. "Not much. The table shook a little. Someone claimed they heard a whisper. Then Evalyn dramatically declared that the spirit world was dormant."

"Well, that's anticlimactic," Erin muttered.

Lauren smiled. "Anyway, I need a few moments in the meditation room before the clients arrive."

As her mother disappeared down the hall, Aubrey turned to Erin. "Do you really think going to a séance will help?"

Erin exhaled slowly. "It's doubtful," she admitted. "But I'm running out of ideas."

Chapter Seven

Strange sounds, a combination of screech and roar, sounded outside the window, waking Padriag from deep slumber. He slipped from the bed, curious to see what happened outside. It was still night, as the moons shone above, turning the sky to dark shades of deep orange and brown. There were no stars in this realm, or perhaps there were, but because of the strange coloring of the sky, they were not visible.

In the distance on a hillside, a herd of auroch made a formidable sight. Two of the beasts lowered their heads and charged toward each other, their massive antlers clashing, the sound almost like thunder.

"What the hell are they doing?" Padriag grumbled. Why didn't the dumb animals fight during the day? It was possible they were nocturnal animals, or that one attacked the other while they slept.

He watched enthralled as the battle continued, now

invested in one of the beasts who was a bit smaller than his opponent.

His door opened and Liam walked in, sword in hand, scanning the room. The Brit came to stand next to him and watched the fight for a moment. "I was wondering what all that noise was." Liam's bedchamber was across the hall, his window facing in the opposite direction. "I thought someone was attacking you."

Another loud screech and roar sounded.

"Do I sound like that when I'm fighting?" Padriag asked.

"Yes, you sound like a wounded beast." Liam turned from the window. "I am going to try to go to the other realm. I hope that this area does not keep us from being able to dematerialize."

"I'm curious to see if it works. I haven't felt any pull to go. If you return, I want to know what happens. If everyone is doing well."

Liam studied him for a long moment. "I will return. As I've said, I plan to continue moving between the realms until you are rescued."

The knight's sacrifice was great, but Padriag knew better than to try to talk him out of it. Liam's honor would not allow him to rest until either Padriag was indeed free or Liam lost the ability to move between the realms. It was Padriag's fear that if that happened, Liam would carry the burden of guilt for years.

"You are aware I don't hold you responsible for killing me. right?" he asked with a grin. "What's murder between friends?"

During a particularly difficult quest that Meliot, the evil

wizard, had set for them, Liam had been forced to pierce Padriag through the heart. Although Liam's ability to see the future had shown that Padriag would live, Liam had no way of knowing if Meliot had tampered with his vision.

Padriag survived, and it became apparent to them that, although Meliot could bring them to the brink of death, they couldn't die. According to the curse, it was only after an imprisonment of three hundred years that would they become mortal, age, and eventually die.

The deadline was imminent and thankfully the other four had been rescued.

"Go," Padriag urged and a scant second later, Liam disappeared.

The clashing of the aurochs sounded again and Padriag closed the shutters. The sounds were muffled, not loud enough to wake him if sleep came, which he doubted.

Flames danced in the hearth casting long shadows across the floor. Studying the mesmerizing movements, Padriag slid onto the bed.

He stared up at the ceiling considering what it would feel like to gain his freedom. When Tristan and then Gavin were rescued, Padriag fully expected to be freed before Niall, who'd insisted he wished to remain behind. Never had he thought to be the last one entrapped and facing life in yet another realm. As thankful as he was for Sterling's hospitality, he would never be part of these people.

Esland would never truly be his home.

. . .

The sound of movement woke him and Padriag opened his eyes just enough to see who it was. One of the servant women was adding a log onto the fire, while another one poured what looked to be tea into a cup from a tray that had been placed atop a table that seemed to serve as a sideboard of sorts.

"Rise in health," the woman pouring the tea greeted, her attention on her task.

Padriag wasn't sure what the proper response was, he would have to ask Sterling. "Thank you."

The woman seemed satisfied with his reply. He watched in silence as they laid clothes out for him and poured steaming water into a basin from a bucket. The silver-haired women spoke to each other in Eslandian, seeming to find something humorous. When they noticed he watched them, they bowed their heads just a bit and hurried from the room.

"I bet they were overcome by my sexiness," Padriag murmured. The probable truth was that the women were curious about his red hair. With everyone looking almost identical there, he'd garnered lots of curiosity.

Once he dressed, Padriag descended to the first level and strolled about while searching for the prince.

"Did you rest well?" Sterling asked when Padriag found him outside. The prince sat at a table with a goblet of some sort of juice. There was a platter of fruit in the center of the table, as well as cuts of meat and cheese.

Sterling motioned to another chair. "Join me for first meal."

"The fighting aurochs woke me," Padriag said. "Do they do that every night?"

A grin spread and Sterling shook his head. "When a young male auroch reaches maturity, the sire challenges him to battle. Usually, the elder wins. It is not a fight to the death, despite how it sounds."

"It sounded like a thunderstorm and a tornado dueling." Padriag leaned forward. "Are there storms here?"

Sterling nodded. "They are called wonders here."

"Your language is nice to hear. Very soft and lilting," Padriag told the prince. "I should learn a bit if I am to stay."

"I can arrange for a tutor," Sterling informed him.

"That would be helpful. I appreciate it. Can I ask, how is it some of you speak English?"

Sterling shrugged. "My sisters and I were taught languages of other realms. Your English, as you call it, is one of them."

They ate in silence for a bit. The juice and fruits tasted different from anything Padriag had ever tasted, but at the same time, it was delicious.

"What keeps you here?" Sterling asked, his gaze locking with Padriag. "What keeps you away from the other realm?"

Ire rose, but Padriag tapped it down. "I want to leave, believe me, I don't want to stay here and die away from my homeland."

"And yet," Sterling said, his attention on the view behind Padriag. "You are not planning to leave. You have resigned yourself to remain here until your death."

What the hell did the man know? "Have you ever left this realm?"

Sterling's iridescent eyes met his, then he looked away. "I have."

"Can you imagine dying away from here? In a place that you didn't know existed. I want to return to the land where I was born. I have been fighting to get out of here."

"I would not wish to be taken from my homeland. I do not wish it for you either." The prince's brow furrowed. "Padriag, you must first release yourself from your burdens. Only then will you be able to allow those who work tirelessly to help you."

"Have you ever seen the Matrix movie?" Padriag asked, sure his smile would annoy Sterling, who stared back blankly. "You remind me of Morpheus."

Padriag was sure the prince had no idea what he was referring to until Sterling chuckled. "I suppose you see yourself as Neo, but I think you're the spoon boy."

"The bald kid that bent silverware. No way. I'm Trinity, she's kick ass." Padriag cocked his head to the side. "How did you watch the movie here?"

Sterling pushed from the table and stood. "I have not watched it, it was forefront in your mind."

He felt his eyes narrow. "Stay out of my head."

"I do. But you sent me the images, wishing me to have something in common with you. Our worlds have more parallels than you can imagine. I must attend to some matters. Enjoy your meal," the prince said, pushing back from the table.

"Talking in riddles is annoying," Padriag called out after him.

LIAM WOKE to find the bed empty, John was already up. He slid from the bed feeling tired. They'd argued the night before over Liam's insistence that he had to spend most of his time in the other realm.

John had not been happy when Liam told him that he and Padriag lived in Esland. "If anything happens to you, I will never know. You are not responsible for Padriag. I'd understand if you went there to check on him, to give messages and such. But you elect to spend your time there and visit here."

Despite Liam's long life, this was his first real relationship. He'd not wanted to be involved with anyone, not until everything was solved. But he was in love with John, could not see life without him. He'd explained it to John, who wasn't convinced.

Upon entering the kitchen, John was pouring a coffee into a second cup and then pushed it to him. "I heard you get up."

Each time Liam saw John, he couldn't keep the lightness in his chest. John was his perfect match. Handsome, quiet, studious, but also passionate.

"I do not wish to argue when I am with you," Liam began. "As far as we know Meliot believes I am still trapped and its imperative he continues to. I will do everything I can to keep my absences shorter. I promise."

John's gaze lifted to his. "Don't make promises you can't keep."

"I made a vow."

Closing the distance, John placed his hands on both sides

of Liam's face. "If we are to continue to be in a relationship, Liam, I want to be a priority."

"Do not leave me," Liam said, a tremble in his voice. "Please."

John's arms came around him and Liam collapsed against him, needing the comfort that only John could give.

"I am doing my best to be patient. But I want you to consider options. Speak to Padriag and the others. Allow yourself to be happy. I want to make you happy."

Unable to form words, Liam took John's mouth with his own, allowing the kiss to convey the depth of the feelings, a caring so deep he was unable to describe it in words.

They would move past it, Liam was sure, it wasn't fair to expect John to stand by while he continued life in the alterworld. At the moment, however, there was no choice.

In truth, Liam wasn't sure of his place if he remained in Scotland. There was nothing for him in England and even if there was, John's life was in Edinburgh. According to Tristan, he'd made arrangements so that Liam was financially well-off, with enough money to live out his days.

But there had to be something to strive for and at the moment, Liam couldn't figure out what it was. In all probability, he was driven by challenges.

Once Padriag was free, traversing a new way of life could be his next challenge. Yes. He would view it as another conquest.

John pushed away and turned back to the stove, where eggs sizzled in a pan. "And just like that, your mind is a hundred miles away." After spooning the eggs over toasted bread, John walked out of the kitchen.

Liam squeezed his eyes shut. If he didn't get himself together, he was going to lose the love of his life.

RIGHT AFTER SHE'D entered the library, Erin felt a wave of relief as John arrived at Dunimarle, though something about him seemed ... off. There was a weight in his posture, a quiet tension in his face that hadn't been there before. Without so much as a greeting, he strode inside, dropped into a chair, and pulled a worn notebook from the crossbody satchel he always carried.

"So, where do we start today?" His voice was clipped, edged with frustration. "I need this whole thing to be over. I hate to admit it, but I'm growing tired of us chasing our tails. Lately, it feels like we're getting nowhere."

Gwen exchanged a glance with Erin before speaking. "I understand your frustration. Your situation is much more complicated than mine or my sisters'." Her tone was gentle, but there was an underlying concern in her eyes. "I just hope the men can convince Liam to limit his time in the other realm."

"He's more useful here than there," Tammie added. "But I get it—he doesn't want Padraig to feel abandoned."

John let out a slow, weary breath, his shoulders sagging as if the weight of everything he carried had finally pressed him down. He nodded in quiet agreement but said nothing, his fingers absently skimming over the edge of his notebook.

Something was gnawing at him. Erin could see it in the shadows beneath his eyes, in the exhaustion carved into the lines of his face. She wondered if he was beginning to lose hope.

Despite her desperate wish to save Padraig, Erin knew she had to agree with the group. Something held Liam tethered to the other realm, as though he wasn't quite ready to return to Scotland. Whether it was unfinished business or sheer reluctance, they couldn't force him.

"Let's try our summoning again," Gwen suggested, glancing at Erin. "This time, with Erin's help. Hopefully, it will work better." She motioned for everyone to hold hands, her expression determined.

Erin took a steadying breath, her fingers threading between the others'. She had memorized the incantation and, as they began to chant in unison, she closed her eyes, willing herself to focus solely on Padraig. The image of him surged to life in her mind—the wild tumble of red waves that cascaded over his broad shoulders, a fiery halo that had intrigued her from the first moment she saw him. She had resisted the urge to sink her fingers into the thick strands, but the temptation had never truly faded.

A deep, rumbling voice broke through the ritual, shattering her concentration.

"Thanks for the party invite. Where's the cake?"

Erin's eyes flew open, her breath catching as she jolted in place.

Padraig stood before them, solid and real, a smirk tugging at his lips.

"Padraig!" Tammie gasped, leaping from her seat. She practically launched herself at him, wrapping her arms around his waist. "You came!"

His hazel-green eyes flicked across the group, assessing each of them in turn, but when they landed on Erin, something in his gaze softened. The smirk deepened.

"Hi, Erin. Nice to see you again."

Her stomach clenched, heat creeping up her neck as an unwelcome shiver ran down her spine. The effect he had on her was nothing short of infuriating. It wasn't just that he was devastatingly handsome—it was the way he unraveled her, stripping away her carefully maintained composure with a single look. She hated feeling so unsteady, so unlike herself, but there was no denying it.

Padraig Clarre affected her in a way she'd never expected. Especially not from a three-hundred-year-old man.

"Let's give them time to talk and figure out things," Tammie said ushering the others from the room.

"We'll be across the hall," Gwen motioned to the doorway as the group filed out of the room.

"Do you mind if we go to the kitchen?" Padraig asked. "I'm hungry for anything from here."

"Sure," Erin replied, standing.

"After you." Padraig motioned for her to walk past.

The pull between them was tangible when she moved closer to the doorway. Then, for some unexplainable reason, she stopped and looked up at him. "If we are to do this, I need to feel more comfortable with you. Can we hug?"

Surprise was evident, his expression instantly changing to what she could only call startled.

"Of course." Padraig opened his arms and Erin cautiously moved into his embrace. Instantly, the familiarity of the last time they'd touched came to mind. It had not been a romantic situation, running for one's life could never be that. But the solid chest, the thick arms and the smell of a combination of leather and meadow reminded her that this man had risked his life for her.

His embrace tightened, and when he pressed a kiss to the side of her head, Erin smiled, glad that she could give him what he'd not had in centuries. Being touched by a woman attracted to him.

"You feel wonderful. I could remain like this forever." His voice, muffled by her hair, sent shivers of delight through her. It would be awkward to be the first to push away, but Erin feared dragging the man to the nearest bed and demanding he take every bit of clothes off.

"I bet there's cake in the kitchen," Erin said, already hating having to move away from him.

Padriag released her, but couldn't seem to stop touching her, his fingers wrapping around her upper arm, his eyes pinned to her face. "That sounds great."

The spacious kitchen was fitted with modern appliances and gleaming marble countertops. A round table with four chairs was surrounded by a bank of floor to ceiling windows. The cook brightened upon seeing them enter. A woman of about forty waved for them to sit, seeming to understand the only reason for them being there was the need to eat.

"I'm starving," Padriag said to the woman, flashing her a smile.

Cook seemed impervious to his attractiveness, then again, she saw the other handsome men, including Gavin, who had to be the most beautiful man on the planet, on a daily basis. "Sit," she instructed.

"I'll start with cake," Padriag said, pointing at what was left of the dessert that was kept on a plate under a glass dome.

The cook not only offered Padriag a slice of cake, but also made Padriag a plate heaping with sausage, roasted tomatoes, potatoes and turnips. The man ate like someone starved for many days. He moaned and closed his eyes, relishing every bite, making Erin smile.

Although left alone in the kitchen, she sensed he didn't want to talk in-depth there. So she asked surface questions.

"How old were you when you left here?"

"Five and twenty."

"What of your family? Did you come from a large family?"

A shadow cross his face, his gaze falling to the table. "Somewhat. I had two siblings, a brother and sister, both older than me," Padriag replied, his tone even. "My parents both came from large families, so I had many aunts, uncles and cousins."

Her heart broke at realizing how hard it must be to outlive your relatives, especially your siblings. She decided to not continue to ask about his family.

"You speak more modernly than the others."

It was nice to see his good-natured grin return. "I came back to Scotland constantly over the years. The changes in the world fascinated me. The others would perhaps wait a decade or two, finding it hard to come knowing they couldn't stay."

"Totally get that," Erin replied. "I am not sure what I'd do in your shoes."

"Since my home was turned into flats, usually younger

people lived there, making it easy for me to keep up with trends and language."

"Being that you are physically young, it would be strange if you spoke like other older people," Erin remarked with a giggle.

He lifted his right eyebrow and looked down his nose at her. "How dare you."

As hard as she tried Erin couldn't stop herself from grinning. "You have such a great sense of humor."

It was cute when he responded with a sheepish shrug.

"We should probably return to the library. I am not sure how long I can remain here." Padriag got up and hurriedly poured a coffee into a large mug. "Don't have this over there."

Once in the library, Erin got her notebook and settled onto the couch. He lowered to sit next to her, leaving a respectable distance between them. When she crossed her legs, he slid a look at her exposed leg. Inevitably, the thought of how long he'd been without sex crossed her mind.

Erin cleared her throat. "I have written down the curse you told to them, but is there more to it?"

His shoulders lifted and lowered. "That is all I remember."

"Can you repeat it for me please?" Erin asked.

Moving his gaze toward the open window, it seemed as if he wished to be anywhere but there in that instant.

Until moon's pale light and dawn's last breath,
I send thee to the brink of death.
Chains of darkness, will not unbind—

Never to be released, your soul, or your mind.

"Interesting." Erin checked her notes, he'd said it word for word, nothing different, but it felt as if the third line stood out to her the most. "Do you feel as if something else, besides the curse, is binding you to the other realm? Is there someone or something that you have reservations about leaving behind?"

Brows lowered, he pondered her question. "I have lived there for a very long time. If you ask if I will miss anything about it, of course I will. To be honest, it feels more like home there than here. I want to leave, I wish to return here, especially now that I do not live at the keep."

"What is the place like. Where you live now?"

As he described an unbelievable world, Erin listened for any changes in tone, for expression of fondness. Nothing stood out.

"What of the people there? Who comes to mind that you will miss when coming here?"

He sucked in his bottom lip in thought, catching her attention, especially when he released it. Padriag had a nice mouth, the bottom lip slightly thicker than the upper.

"I am not going to miss anyone. Other than the men I grew close with, the only other people I know are Sterling, his sisters, and, I suppose evil Meliot. I most certainly will not miss him."

Erin had so many questions written down, she skipped some to ask the ones she figured would help. "What do you look forward to the most about coming here?"

The wicked grin and darkening of his eyes when looking

at her, made the answer very evident. Erin felt her eyes widen and her cheek redden. "Other than that. What else?"

"Food, the fresh air of Scotland, being with my friends, seeing them marry and all of us grow old." He stopped and cleared his throat. "Oh there are cars now, so driving will be great."

She wondered where he would get income from. After all, he would be in a new world without any marketable trade, but it wasn't important at the moment. "I was told you have some magical abilities. Have you tried to sense answers to breaking the curse?"

"I have tried so many things. Not just for myself, but also for the others. But nothing ever worked. My magic is limited to protective wards, invisibility, and lighting. I can make things float, but that's pretty useless."

"Does it work here?" Erin leaned forward. "Can I see it?"

Padriag shrugged. "I have never tried it here."

"How about we try together. I have no abilities, but for some reason the group across the hall think I am the one chosen to rescue you."

"Do you have a spell yet?" Padriag asked.

Erin nodded. "The start of one. It's not finished. At least I do not think it is." She held out her hands. "Try your magic, maybe see if you can weave a ward around us. I will chant the spell."

When they held hands, it suddenly felt silly. Casting a spell wasn't something Erin ever thought to do, especially not with a witness.

"Relax and trust," Padriag said, his eyes meeting hers. "You have to believe it for it to work."

It had to work. If she was chosen for this, it was up to her, and she had to try hard. Taking a deep breath, Erin closed her eyes.

The warding spell was easy to sense, it was as if the air was filled with static electricity, gently sizzling but not feeling threatening.

In a soft voice, Erin called to the spirits as she'd been taught by John. "Come spirits of light, hear me, help me. I await you, come spirits in your power."

She waited unsure if it had worked or not. Padriag squeezed her hands, and she began the spell she'd written.

"By love unbroken, by bond unshaken,
I summon the heart that fate has taken.
Break these chains, undo the night,
Return, my knight, to truth and light."

When she began repeating the spell, the room spun, and she found it hard to stay seated. Losing Padriag's hold, Erin was tossed from the sofa and landed on the floor. Unable to see as everything became dark, she heard a thud, followed by Padriag's curse.

"Shit. I banged my head."

There was nothing different about the room, other than one of the sofa pillows on the floor, Padriag lying next to the fireplace and Erin on the rug.

"What happened?" Gwen exclaimed, running into the room, John and Tammie behind her.

"I think Erin may be on the right track with her spell,"

Padriag said, jumping to his feet and hurrying to help Erin up. "Something didn't want her to finish."

"That's amazing," Tammie said, hands clutched in front of her chest.

The women and John sat around the table once again, going over the spell and trying to figure out what, if anything, needed to be added or changed.

Padriag, who'd spent most of the time pacing, came up to Erin and placed his hand on her shoulder. "I have to go back now. Can I speak to you privately?"

"Of course." Erin stood and together they went outside.

He glanced around and took a deep breath. "Strange how the air smells differently here. The scent is so familiar, it feels good to inhale it.

Reaching for her hand, he brought it up to his lips, kissed the back of it, and then held it with both of his.

"Erin, thank you. I don't dare hope for freedom. I sense that I may not be freed. Yet, I greatly appreciate everything that you and the others are doing."

Struck silent, Erin wasn't sure what to think. They'd just made progress, why was Padriag so convinced that he'd not be able to break his curse.

When she looked up at him, his gaze fell as he seemed to struggle for words.. "When the time comes, I believe you will know it. Please stop trying. Go back to living your life. I can't ask you to continue this indefinitely. It's not fair to you." He looked toward the house. "And it is not fair to them. I do ask one thing of you, do your best to convince the others that I have accepted my fate."

"I-I don't understand," Erin stammered. "Why are you

so convinced it won't work. Everything they have been doing, it's working. What happened today, that is definitely progress. You even said ..."

"What everyone needed to hear. The way we were thrown off, means the spell did not work and will not work. It is the wrong one. If there is a spell to break the curse, I doubt you or anyone can find it."

"I can't give up. Not now," Erin replied, her voice barely above a whisper.

Padriag shook his head. "I best go."

To her utter surprise and delight, he took her in his arms and kissed her. Erin returned the kiss, wrapping her arms around his neck, melting against him.

Mine.

The word slammed into her mind. More than a thought, or a wish, it was a sense that he was to be hers. Padriag would not be left behind. She felt it in her bones.

"Padriag." Her words sounded husky as she spoke into his ear. "I am not giving up."

His mouth took hers once again, and he pulled her close. Then he broke away, his eyes locked with hers until he dematerialized and was gone.

Chapter Eight

The air shifted around him as Padriag materialized in the labyrinth at Sterling's castle. Relieved not to have appeared outside the gates, he bent at the waist in relief. The entire time he'd been at Dunimarle, he'd worried about the return to Esland.

There was no telling what would have occurred if he'd miscalculated and ended up in a place from where it would be hard to traverse without being poisoned by plants or killed by whatever creatures were out there.

He made his way into the castle and climbed the stairs toward the rooms he and Liam had been assigned.

"Padriag," Sterling called from the first floor. "We must speak."

The prince's expression was grim. Either he'd done something wrong, or there was bad news considering the tight line his lips formed.

"With me," Sterling said, motioning for Padriag to

accompany him. Together they walked into what looked to be the prince's private dining room.

Once inside, Sterling turned sharply to face him, his silver-blue eyes unreadable in the dim candlelight. "We should sit."

Padriag swallowed against the knot tightening in his stomach. The prince's tone, clipped and formal, gave him little doubt that whatever was about to be said wouldn't be good. Still, he followed him in silence to a balcony where a small, ornately carved table sat beneath the open sky. The night air carried the scent of jasmine and something metallic —perhaps the lingering aura of Esland's strange foliage.

They sat. The tension between them was palpable. Sterling's fingers drummed against the polished surface of the table, his expression one of barely concealed impatience.

"Is there anything you wish to say to me?" the prince asked, his voice deceptively calm.

Not exactly the way Padriag had expected this conversation to begin. He frowned. "About?"

"Today."

Padriag exhaled slowly, keeping his expression neutral. "I wasn't around much today. I came down, had first meal, then returned to my room, changed clothes, and attempted to cross into the other realm. For the past few weeks, it has been nearly impossible. Today, it was ... easier. Judging by the movement of the suns in the sky, I was gone for half a day."

Sterling's frown deepened, his fingers stilling. "I am certain that when Veylen explained our laws to you and Liam, he made it abundantly clear—Esland forbids travel outside the realm."

Padriag's brow lifted. "So your citizens are prisoners?"

The reaction was immediate. The prince's nostrils flared, and his gaze darkened with cold fury. "They are protected, not imprisoned," he ground out, his grip tightening on the arms of his chair. "If they wish to leave, they may do so."

"If they manage to survive what you claim to be a poisonous and perilous wasteland." Padriag's tone was measured but laced with challenge. "And I assume, should they succeed, they are considered outcasts?"

Sterling's lips pressed into a thin line, his jaw tightening. "Do not pretend to understand the laws of my kingdom."

It took every ounce of restraint not to push further. Padriag had already tested the prince's temper enough and antagonizing him would get him nowhere. Instead, he inclined his head slightly.

"I will allow it just this once," Sterling said after a long pause, his tone firm. "Perhaps you did not fully grasp the information when it was first explained to you."

Padriag nodded, his expression schooled into something more diplomatic. "When Veylen told us that travel to the other realms was forbidden, we understood it to mean to Atlandia or Meliot's gloomy lands—not that we were barred from dematerializing and returning home."

Some of the fire in Sterling's gaze dimmed, and his posture eased. "That is why I am forgiving this time."

But Padriag understood now—Esland's laws were meant not only for its citizens, but for visitors as well. He and Liam were no exceptions.

A heavy silence stretched between them before he spoke again, his voice calm but unwavering. "According to your law, once someone leaves this realm, they cannot return." He met Sterling's gaze directly. "Once Liam returns, we will leave and return to the other realm, Atlandia, or where our keep is. There is no choice but to take our chances with Meliot's sentries."

Sterling said nothing.

Padriag pressed on. "The only way for me to be freed is to be in Scotland when it happens. Every one of our group whose curse has been broken was in the other realm."

He took a breath before continuing. "Sterling, do you truly intend for me to remain here for the rest of my life? To be a burden, someone who depends on you and your hospitality until death?"

The prince's expression was unreadable once more. Then, in a voice as smooth and unwavering as steel, he said, "You are welcome to remain here as long as you wish. My hospitality has no other limitations."

Padriag clenched his jaw, his heart pounding. A gilded cage was still a cage. And it seemed that Sterling had no intention of wavering when it came to his ability to travel between Esland and Scotland.

Servants entered and quietly placed a tray before them which held what looked to be a tea pot along with two empty cups and a pair of plates with a baked pastry.

A women poured the dark liquid, while the other, a man lifted the plates and placed them in front of the prince and then Padriag.

Sterling waved them away wordlessly. Both ignored the offerings.

"I appreciate your hospitality If we'd understood your laws, we would have declined the offer."

"You speak for Liam Murray. How do you know he agrees?"

It seemed that Prince Sterling had never been part of a team but had a solitary life. Those surrounding him were there because he was ruler. His only family, the ruling sisters of Atlandia, lived in another realm. From what Padriag had seen over the years, the siblings rarely communicated.

"Liam has ties to our homeland, Scotland. He is in a relationship, tied to another and will never agree to the prohibition of travel between the realms. Despite the fact that he can remain there, he chooses to travel back here to ensure my well-being."

"As I said. You are welcome to remain here as long as you wish. If it is to be the rest of your life, so be it. This can be your home." The Prince leaned back and looked out to the view.

Admittedly, Esland was wild and beautiful. The pleasing sounds of the waterfalls, the misting water and rainbows reminded Padriag of kingdoms described in fairytales.

"For centuries, I have fought for my people's safety," the prince said, breaking Padriag away from studying the landscape. The prince's attention remained directed past him toward the village.

"When I was a young boy, Esland was a huge realm, many times the size of the land now with a far larger amount of people."

"What happened?" Padriag asked.

Keeping his face turned away, Sterling continued. "Our

borders were not protected then. A people of peace, there never was a need for any army. My parents, they never got along. Father ruled over Esland and Mother over Atlandia. It was that way for many centuries."

He was silent for a moment, as if assessing how to proceed. When he spoke again, his tone was grave. "Meliot's father was killed. Many say it was the dark wizard himself who killed him in order to absorb his sire's powers. In Meliot's bloodline, the powers pass to whomever kills them. I am not sure of all the intricacies of the Dark Realm. One thing I do know is that after his sire's death, Meliot became powerful, able to create an army of virtually indestructible warriors. Attacks on Atlandia and Esland decimated our people and our resources."

"How did you survive?" Padriag was truly intrigued about how the kingdoms survived the wars.

"Dragons," Sterling replied. "During my wanderings, I went into a cave where I had found a dying dragon with two hatchlings. I brought the mother and hatchlings fruit and small beasts, doing my best to help. She recovered and was able to keep watch over her young. I didn't see them again for years. I was afraid they'd see me as a meal."

The prince smiled while speaking, seeming fond of those moments. "When I was a very young warrior, a boy still really, the mother dragon often flew over where I rode. After a while, the other warriors became accustomed to her presence. She defended me from death many times.

"Then one day, she landed and waited for me to come near. I understood I was to ride her. From then on, we have become inseparable."

The story wasn't at all what Padriag had thought when first seeing Sterling with his dragon. "Is she still alive?"

"Yes, she is Amai, my dragon. The one who saved you from Meliot's castle," Sterling replied, referring to when Meliot had taken Tammie and Erin captive just before Niall was rescued.

"So the others, the ones flying around here are all her children?"

Sterling nodded. "They are."

Dragons took at least ten years to reach maturity, which meant the war waged on until the prince was a full-grown man. Strange that Sterling was a warrior, from Padriag's experience, royalty was usually shielded from true danger.

Padriag was enthralled.

Sterling shook his head. "The dragons defended both Esland and Atlandia, they killed many of the dark forces, but in the end, we lost huge portions of our lands to the dark mists."

"Why is Esland still separate from Atlandia?" Padriag asked since the prince seemed in a mood to share.

"When the war ended things changed. My sisters were resentful that I didn't give their realm dragons. As much as I tried to explain that dragons are territorial and would always return to Esland, they didn't understand, insisting it was my choice."

"So the dark mists belong to Meliot?" Padriag inquired.

Prince Sterling shook his head. "Once dark mists took over an area, it became uninhabitable to anyone, including Meliot's dark forces.

"Look." Sterling pointed to the distance. "From here you can see where Esland ends."

Indeed past the mountains at the edges, what seemed to be dark smoke, or mist rose from the ground, creating a hazy wall.

"I say all this," Sterling continued, "so that you understand. I am not trying to keep my people captive. Many remember the darkness taking over. Many lost entire families to the mist. They want to be safe. Letting people come and go from our realm could make us vulnerable."

"I understand," Padriag replied. "More than you know."

"So we leave. Perhaps we can go to Atlandia. Ask the princesses for asylum." Liam let out an indignant snort. "I understand why he has such strict rules, but surely he knows we would never cause harm to the realm."

"Nothing to do about it, he is inflexible." Padriag pointed at Liam. "Please go back. Stay there. You can pop back once I'm settled elsewhere. There really is no need for you guard me, or whatever you think to be doing. It's annoying."

The Brit looked up to the ceiling, his jaw muscle tightening. "I made a vow to keep you safe."

"I already told you. I am over the whole killing me incident. As you can see, fully healed with only a scar that's pretty sexy."

"I'm going to sleep." Liam turned towards his room.

"Wait," Padriag called out, not ready for his friend to

leave. "Since you spent time with the others ... anything I should know?"

He tried to keep his voice neutral, devoid of the yearning that gnawed at his insides, but it was a losing battle. The ache of separation had settled deep in his bones. It was inevitable. For centuries, he had lived side by side with Tristan, Gavin, Niall, and Liam—fought with them, laughed with them, bled with them. Now, the absence of their familiar presence left an emptiness so vast, some mornings he awoke expecting to hear their voices drifting through the halls, the distant sound of Niall's hammering on whatever project he worked on, the scrape of boots on stone. But the silence met him instead, and it was deafening.

Liam turned, his expression unreadable in the dim light. "They are well," he said evenly, but there was an undertone of something heavier in his voice. "And, as expected, quite worried about your plight." He hesitated, as if choosing his next words carefully. "They urged me to tell you that no one has given up hope, and that they will battle for as long as it takes to find a way to free you."

A tightness coiled in Padriag's chest. Of course, he had never doubted them—not for a single moment. They were bound not just by time, but by something far deeper, their brotherhood. And yet, it pained him to know they would waste their days chasing a lost cause. He would have done the same if the roles were reversed, but that didn't make it easier to accept.

He exhaled slowly, running a hand over his face before meeting Liam's gaze. "Once we leave Esland, please Liam, return to Scotland." His voice was firm, steady, though every part of him wished he didn't have to say it. "I mean it, Liam. Go to John. He may not be as patient as he's been for much longer."

Liam's expression hardened, his jaw clenching as if bracing for a fight. "Then he is not the person for me," he bit out, his tone defiant. Without waiting for a response, he turned away, his shoulders tense.

Padriag knew that wasn't the truth. He and Liam had been friends long enough to see through each other's facades, and this was no different. Liam cared—perhaps more than he was willing to admit—but he was stubborn. Loyal to a fault. And though Padriag appreciated it, he couldn't let it continue.

Keeping his voice even, he pressed on. "If I am to stay behind, I need to get used to it. I must start life on my own, not depending on you to be here. Because the day will come when you won't be able to." He let the words settle, hoping they would sink in. "You and I both know that day is coming. May as well let it begin now."

Liam remained rigid, unmoving. The fire in the hearth crackled softly, the only sound between them for a long, weighted moment. Finally, without turning around, Liam spoke, his voice quieter now. "Go to sleep. We have much to do tomorrow."

Padriag exhaled, knowing the conversation was over—for now. But the words had been spoken, and they would linger, just as the ghosts of his old life did.

He went to a chair and leaned back, staring at the ceiling, wondering how long it would take before he truly believed the things he had just said.

. . .

Sterling was absent at first meal. Undoubtedly, he expected that Padriag would inform Liam of the conversation they'd had about Esland laws.

The meal was flavorful, but unusual. There was a sort of porridge, slices of meat, which Padriag guessed to be native to Esland as well as tea that tasted somewhat like coffee. A bread-like item was served in a loaf from which they could tear chunks. It tasted like wood chips to Padriag, but he figured the more he ate, the better suited he'd be physically for leaving the realm.

"I don't think the outskirts of Atlandia are far from here." Liam studied the food on the table, as if deciphering the contents. "Hopefully we can reach the small village just outside Atlandia and the people will remember us."

Heavy footfalls sounded, Veylen appeared and joined them. Not bothering with a greeting, the warrior piled food on his plate and began eating.

"Good Rising to you," Padriag said in a jovial tone.

Veylen gave him a wry look. "We cannot escort you to the border today. Perhaps in a day or two. There is a matter of urgency on our northern border." He continued eating, refilling his plate, obviously preparing for battle and perhaps long days with little to eat.

"Is there anything we can do to help?" Liam, forever a knight, asked.

"Doubtful," Veylen replied, his accessing gaze moving over Liam. "Your offer is appreciated."

At least the man had manners, Padriag thought.

"Liam is an accomplished cook. He can come along and ensure the men are fed," Padriag offered. "I would offer my sword but am unsure of fighting from the back of an auroch. I'm sure I can learn quickly."

"I do not cook," Liam said in a clipped tone. "Besides their food is unlike anything we've ever eaten."

Padriag grinned. "You can be a sous chef to whoever the cook is."

"Shut up." Liam lifted the tea to his lips and took a long sip. "This is a serious matter, not a time for you to jest."

"Hey, trying to help as you are so keen on going to battle, or whatever they are going to the northern border to do."

Veylen shook his head. "We are prepared for battle, but it is doubtful it will come to that. Your presence would hinder and not help."

Picturing the realm borders, Padriag tried to think what lands were north to Esland. He'd assumed it was the mists.

"Sterling told me you were surrounded by mists on the sides not on the Atlandia border." Padriag studied Veylen, who's face shuttered.

The warrior pushed back from the table. "As I said, it may be several days before escort can be arranged." With that he walked from the room.

"If we had horses, we could leave on our own," Liam said leaning back. "I suppose a few days reprieve gives us time to plan better."

It was true, but their options were limited. Other than heading to Atlandia, there was nowhere else to go. Unlike the villagers there, Padraig was not physically able to survive the icing storms that occurred almost daily. How those people managed to grow food and keep livestock alive was a testament to their tenacity.

"Do you remember that mountain not too far from the keep?" Padriag asked, picturing the location of one of their quests when they'd chased a dragon. "If I recall correctly, there was a village up there. The weather is better and maybe I can negotiate living there in exchange for something. Protection, magic, shit I don't know."

Liam nodded. "I do remember it. Believe it to be called Briaga, the people seemed accepting. You can offer to be the village idiot."

"I could, but my wit is too sharp for most, and they'd quickly vote me as their leader. I am not prepared for the responsibility," Padriag quipped. "What about blacksmithing? Niall taught me quite a bit."

"If there is a need for one in the village, one is probably already there." Liam shook his head. "I am sure you can make do. You are quick on your feet."

Visions of wearing torn rags and begging for food swarmed through his mind, and Padriag shook them off. This was not the time for negative thinking.

At the sharp cries echoing through the air, the two men jolted upright and rushed onto the balcony. Below, a formation of nearly a hundred warriors sat astride massive, horned aurochs, their muscular frames shifting beneath gleaming armor. The enormous beasts bellowed, nostrils flaring as they pawed the earth, their breath misting in the crisp morning air. From every window and balcony, people leaned out, waving vibrant cloths of crimson, gold, and emerald, their voices rising in rhythmic chants that pulsed like a heartbeat through the city.

Above them, the sounds of the powerful sweep of dragon wings. A dozen great beasts circled, their scales catching the light, flashing hues of deep sapphire, fiery copper, and obsidian black. But among them, one stood out—a breathtaking iridescent dragon, its shimmering scales reflecting a rainbow of shifting colors. Atop its powerful back sat Sterling, his silhouette regal against the dawn.

Though other dragons loomed larger, their forms more fearsome, none could rival the ethereal beauty of Sterling's mount. The dragon let out a piercing, bone-shaking screech, its throat swelling before it unleashed a torrent of flames—blazing ribbons of orange and red that streaked across the sky.

At the command, the Eslandian army surged forward in unison, their mounts' huge hooves like thunder as they headed northward.

Chapter Nine

Flames of what had to be at least twenty candles scattered around the cramped room provided the only light. Erin shifted in her chair refusing to look at Aubrey. If they made eye contact, one or both of them would burst out laughing. Instead, she looked to the others instead of her cousin. Evalyn, dressed in a long dark purple caftan presided from an ornate chair, her hands held palms up as she chanted what sounded like gibberish. There was a mother-daughter pair who'd pronounced they wanted to hear from the mother's recently deceased husband, and a woman who looked to be over eighty seeking to communicate with her long-departed sister.

Erin had reported the need to communicate with a dead man named Padriag, who'd been a knight in the sixteen hundreds. Unable to think of anyone dead, Aubrey said she was there to support Erin's research.

Despite feeling this was not going to help the quest for

the spell that would break Padriag free from the curse, Erin found she was enjoying the spectacle.

"Rosa! Who do you wish to speak to?" Evalyn asked in a theatrical voice. "Who are you?"

When the others were silent, Evalyn tilted her head. "Repeat your name, tell me who you are?"

It may have been Erin's imagination, but just then a breeze swept past shifting the candle's flames to one side.

"Rosemarie," Evalyn amended. "Who do you wish to speak to?"

"That's my sister," the elderly woman exclaimed, her eyes going wide. "What is she saying?"

"Shhh!" Evalyn hissed. "Wait. Oh yes. Yes." There was a long silence and then Evalyn's head fell backward. Lifting her head, she spoke. "Rosemarie says hello and that she is well."

"Oh." The older woman sounded disappointed. "Is that all?"

Evalyn shrugged and closed her eyes again. "Rosemarie, do you have a message for your sister?" Once again after a moment her head flopped, this time to her chest. Slowly, she looked up at the elderly woman. "She's still mad over you kissing Henry Whittle. But he's there now and you can't get to him."

"Henry's dead?" The elderly woman's mouth fell open. "I'll have to send a card to the family."

There was no communication between the mother-daughter and their dead one. Evalyn told them he was still in the process of transitioning and was busy learning how to be in the other plane. Erin couldn't help but picture there being some sort of in-processing center for those recently dead along with long video presentations about their new existence.

"You are next," Evalyn announce motioning to Erin. "This Padriag, how is he part of your life?"

"I date, er, am dating one of his decedents and he mentioned that anyone who was to be with him long-term would have to be accepted by his great-great-great-grandfather, Padriag Clarre."

"Ah," Evalyn said, as if it was the most normal of things. "I see." She frowned and added. "Since he's been dead for so long, I ask that everyone assist in this. Join hands, close your eyes and repeat what I say in your mind."

Everyone did as they were told, and Erin felt a pang of guilt for lying. At the same time, she was poised in case something came to her. Perhaps just being there would give her inspiration to write something. To add to the spell she was working on.

Evalyn let out a dramatic breath. "Spirits of beyond. You are welcome here. Speak. We summon Padriag of many years past. Come forth. You are safe here."

Despite having her eyes closed, Erin tried to roll them at how silly it all was, but she resisted and forced herself to relax.

"It is you." The voice was masculine, deep and guttural. Everyone gasped, someone let out a yelp, and they all opened their eyes and gawked at Evalyn. Her face was taut, open eyes, completely black, moved from face to face. Each of the people around the table shrank back, eyes wide, mouths agape.

"Hello Erin."

Immediately Erin recognized who spoke. It was Meliot,

the evil wizard from the alter-world. She'd been told he could not inhabit this realm. Yet somehow the evil being was here, his malevolence tangible. Terror and dread seized every part of her body as memories returned, being forcibly taken to the other realm, imprisoned in his dark castle and threatened. Every moment so vivid, it was as if she was back there, not knowing if she'd ever see her loved ones again. A whimper escaped as she tried her best not to cry.

The black eyes focused on her. "His fate is sealed. There is nothing strong enough to break the bonds I have placed keeping Padriag in my world."

Leaning back as far as she could, Erin slid a look to Aubrey, whose eyes were round as saucers, her breaths coming in short pants.

"I-I will n-not g-give up," Erin stuttered, unable to keep the shaking from her voice. Immediately, warning bells rung loudly in her head against saying anything more.

Evalyn's lips curved into a twisted smile that was not her own. "Do you wish to trade your soul for one already damned? Are you willing to sacrifice everything to me? Take his place. Suffer his torment?" Evalyn's eyelids lowered then lifted, the black abyss of her gaze digging into Erin's.

Too stunned to speak, she jumped when his cackle echoed around the room and half of the candle flames were doused. "I didn't think so. Turn away now. Do nothing more or pay the consequences. Stop your useless feeble attempts unless you wish to be bound to me as well." What felt like an ice-cold finger trailed down the side of her neck, Erin gasped leaning away. Her lungs seized with terror, and she began shaking uncontrollably.

"Don't touch me," she cried out.

Everyone turned to look at her. Erin was sure she'd turned as white as a ghost.

Coughs got everyone's attention, Evalyn was hunched over hacking and gulping in air. Aubrey moved the woman's glass of water closer to her. With a shaky hand Evalyn reached for it and gulped half of the contents down as everyone watched in silence.

Sliding glances around the table and seeing the pale faces and tense expressions, Erin gathered that everyone was still anxious and fearful.

"Wh-what happened?" Evalyn gasped out the words, reaching for her cigarettes. She lit one and looked at each person in turn. "Well?"

"I think you were possessed by something evil," the elderly woman explained. "Your eyes turned black, and you were really ugly."

"I wouldn't say that," the mother of the duo stated, giving Evalyn a cautious look. "Just a bit malevolent."

"Malevolent?" Evalyn shrieked, repeating the word. She glared at Erin. "Was your boyfriend's great-great-great-whatever into dark magic?"

The elderly woman held up a gnarled finger. "He was like the devil himself. Dear me, I think I wet my pants."

"We're leaving." The mother-daughter duo hurried to their feet, threw money on the table and rushed out.

Aubrey, Erin, and Evalyn turned to the elderly woman. She shrugged. "I am staying. This is better than the telly."

"What do you have to say?" Evalyn eyes snapped to Erin. "You got me possessed."

"I did not," Erin said, unable to think of how to get out of the current mess. "You invited him ... it. Asked if it had something to say."

"Did you recognize the evil spirit?" Aubrey asked but then pressed her lips together when Erin gave her a pointed look.

Not to be dissuaded, Evalyn narrowed her gaze. "Go on then. Tell us. Who was it?"

"I-I don't know. But the spirit warned me off. I suppose it means I did not meet their expectations for a partner to their great-great-great-grandson."

The elderly woman bit into a cookie. "Said your boyfriend is damned or doomed. It's probably a good thing you got rejected."

"We'd best go. Sorry about that," Erin said to Evalyn. "How much do I owe you?"

"Don't worry about it. Just make sure to tell others about this experience. Do not leave out the black eyes." By the way Evalyn's expression suddenly changed, a gleam in her eyes, she saw monetary potential from the experience.

Evalyn grabbed the money from the table and shoved it into her bra. "I suppose those two will spread the word. Everyone will know I am a real medium." She grinned and turned her attention to the elderly lady. "Lavinia. Tell everyone at the senior manor about this."

"I'm almost ninety, who the hell do you think will believe me?" Lavinia snapped, then seemed to reconsider. "Then again, most of the people we knew are dead. So it can be good business. Do I get a cut? If they believe me, that is."

"Someone will, I am sure of it," Aubrey, ever the soft heart told the old woman.

Evalyn nodded. "Of course Lavinia and you can talk to your sister whenever you want. Now let's get you home. Let me get a towel to put on the seat." Evalyn walked out and return within seconds with a towel.

"I wet my underpants," Lavinia informed Erin and Aubrey. "Did I mention it?"

"You did," Erin and Aubrey chorused.

"That was unsettling," Aubrey muttered once they were safely ensconced in Erin's car. She rubbed her arms as if warding off an unseen chill. "Who was that?"

Erin swallowed against the lingering unease curling in her gut. "Meliot." Even saying the name felt like summoning evil. She trembled, gripping the steering wheel tighter. "How in the world did he do it? From what the others have told me, he can't touch anyone in this realm." And yet, he was there—real enough to make her skin crawl, his presence as real as if he'd been there in the flesh.

Aubrey's voice trembled. "What are you going to do now?"

"Talk to the others. Explain what happened."

"We should sleep at my place tonight," Aubrey suggested, glancing over her shoulder as though expecting something—someone—to jump up and scare them.

Erin nodded, her thoughts a storm of worry and exhaustion. "In the morning, we'll go to the castle. I'll call Mum and ask her to take my morning class." Her voice shook just enough that Aubrey gave her a concerned look.

They rode in tense silence, the quiet of the night pressing in around them. The rhythmic hum of the tires on the road was oddly comforting. When they finally turned onto the estate's long drive, Erin exhaled, her shoulders easing as Ashcraig Hall, a beautiful stone home, came into view.

The sight of it washed over her like balm. Memories stirred, a childhood spent racing across the sprawling lawns, climbing trees in spite of scraped knees, and sneaking into the kitchens for stolen sweets. Since her birth, she and her parents had lived there until the long commute to the city became too much, prompting them to settle in a smaller home in Edinburgh. But the estate had never stopped being a second home. Weekends had still been spent at Ashcraig Hall, their quarters kept just like they'd left them.

Now, only Aubrey lived here, but the house remained full of promise. Erin and Aubrey planned to share the home one day, raising their children together in the historical setting. The thought should have been comforting. Tonight, it only felt fragile.

"Can I sleep in your room?" Erin asked, her voice quieter than before. "I'm still a bit shaky."

Aubrey didn't hesitate. "I was going to suggest it if you didn't. I don't want to be alone either." She pushed open the car door, the creak of the hinges sounding louder than usual.

Erin followed suit, stepping into the cool night air. She made sure to lock the car out of habit, though it was highly unlikely anyone would come all the way up a secluded private drive just to steal her ten-year-old vehicle.

And yet, as they walked toward the house, the sensation of being watched prickled along Erin's spine.

DESPITE SHARING the large bed with Aubrey, Erin couldn't relax. Her restless tossing and turning kept her cousin from sleeping as well, earning a few annoyed sighs from the other side of the mattress. When Aubrey's breathing finally settled into the soft, rhythmic pattern of sleep, Erin slipped from the bed, careful not to wake her, and padded toward the kitchen. A hot toddy—cinnamon tea with honey and a splash of whiskey—would do the trick.

She rarely took pills unless the pain was unbearable, but dousing tea with alcohol wasn't exactly a wholesome alternative. Still, the warmth and effect of the drink sounded perfect.

Making her way down the dimly lit corridor, her ears strained for anything out of place. The old house, built of sturdy stone and brick, had its share of familiar sounds—the groan of aged wood, the occasional pop of settling beams, the whisper of tree branches scraping against the windows. Those who'd lived there had grown accustomed to the natural symphony of Ashcraig Hall. And yet, Erin was certain she'd recognize the moment something didn't belong.

Her phone's flashlight cast long, eerie shadows against the walls. Every few steps, she paused, holding her breath and listening. Each time, she felt foolish and continued forward, reminding herself there was nothing to fear.

The kitchen, spacious and steeped in history, welcomed her with its familiar comforts. Like many homes of its kind, a large picture window overlooked the back garden, and a glass-paned door led into the conservatory. In daylight, the view was lovely, rows of flourishing herbs, a tangle of roses climbing trellises, and beyond that, the wilder sprawl of the land. Even at night, Ashcraig Hall filled her with a sense of belonging. A future here wasn't just possible—it was something she longed for.

As the kettle whistled, she prepared her tea, stirring in honey and a generous splash of whiskey before settling at the table. Her thoughts drifted back to the wizard's warning. The memory of his voice sent a shiver coursing through her, the cold edge of his words lingering like a shadow in her mind. How far did his punishments truly go? The freed men spoke in hushed tones of horrors she had only caught fragments of. Were his threats real, or simply meant to terrify?

If only she could speak to Padriag. He would know. He could tell her whether Meliot's warnings were mere intimidation or something far worse.

Determined not to forget a single detail, Erin pulled open a drawer, retrieving a pad of paper and a pen. She scrawled out the wizard's words, careful to capture them precisely. Then, as the quiet house pressed in around her, she let her thoughts spill onto the next page—half-formed ideas, tangled fears, scattered possibilities.

By the time she glanced down, two pages were filled. Most of it was likely useless, but somewhere in the ink and frantic scribbles, she hoped to find the answers.

"Wow," a male voice said.

Erin jumped and let out a yelp, the tea sloshing over the

cup's brim onto her hand, then splashing onto the tabletop. Thankfully it had cooled enough that it didn't burn.

Padriag stood at the kitchen entrance, looking around with a frown. "Well this is unexpected."

"How are you here? I don't think I called for you," Erin sputtered.

A bit disheveled, Padriag wore an unbelted tan colored tunic that hung to just above his knees. His silken red hair poked out in all directions, and he rubbed his eyes and yawned as if he'd been roused from a deep sleep.

His wide shoulders lifted and lowered. "I have no idea. Wait, is this a dream?" Walking closer to Erin, he pinched her arm.

"Ouch," Erin rubbed the spot and glared at him. "You are supposed to pinch yourself." In actuality, it had not hurt. Unsettled by his presence, she stood and reached for a kitchen towel to clean up the spilled tea, needing to do something to keep from doing something stupid like throwing herself into his arms and confessing how scared she was.

"Where are we?" Padriag asked through another wide yawn. "It's a nice kitchen."

"Ashcraig Hall, my family home," Erin replied. "It is and has always been a beautiful home. Aubrey, my cousin, lives here at the moment." She let out a breath. "I came here tonight because I was afraid to be alone."

Immediately his countenance changed, and he moved closer. "Did something happen?"

Tears threatened and Erin blew out a breath. "Would you like something to eat? Drink?"

Padriag shook his head. "Not right now. Thank you. Tell me what occurred."

Her legs felt shaky, Erin blinked away tears. "Its best we go to the other room. I need to sit down."

Once in the adjoining room, she lowered to a sofa and Padriag joined her. "Tell me what happened." He took her hand, and she was surprised how comforting it was.

"I went to a séance, Aubrey and I, we both went. Honestly, I didn't expect anything to come from it. But something did." Erin continued on, telling Padriag what happened at Evalyn's house and exactly what the entity she assumed was Meliot had said through the woman.

The entire time, Padriag listened in silence, his expression unreadable.

"That may be the reason I am here. As you can probably tell, I was asleep. Don't think anyone else has ever traveled between realms while sleeping."

"What should we do?" Erin asked. "It was terrifying. Each time I think about it, I feel vulnerable."

Padriag looked to be thinking, a frown marring his brow, lips flat. "You shouldn't be alone. I agree with that. However, Meliot cannot cause physical harm in this realm. His ability to speak through someone here means his powers have increased somewhat. Doing what he did is not much more than a parlor trick."

"What about the warning?"

"I must speak to the others." He looked to the windows. "I assume it's the middle of the night here."

Erin nodded, she stood and paced, nervous energy not allowing for her to remain still. His effect on her was strong.

It felt impossible to keep from reaching out to touch him constantly.

Clearing her throat, she spoke. "Aubrey and I planned to go to Dunimarle Castle and speak to the others first thing in the morning. Hopefully, between all of us, we can decipher what it all means." The entire time, she knew he followed her movement, his gaze steadily on her, which made her even more nervous.

When she slid a look toward him, he didn't look away. The normally light green and amber eyes darkening as he met hers. "You are beautiful." His lips curved and he shrugged. "Had to say it."

"Thank you." Erin's cheeks warmed.

"I will go with you to see the others. He motioned to his tunic and bare legs. Would you happen to have any pants around, maybe shoes?"

Despite the situation, Erin giggled. "Not that I know of. We can ask Aubrey in the morning. It's doubtful. You may have to stay as is until we get to Dunimarle."

Erin yawned. "It best we get some rest. Come. I'll show you a bedchamber." She stood and he did as well. "Unless you are going back to the other realm to get clothes and returning in the morning."

"I will stay here. Whatever Meliot is up to, we must see about it immediately." He looked at the short sofa. "I can sleep here."

"There are eight bedrooms in this house. Mine is on this floor, and there is another also on this floor."

"Stay with me," Padriag said, his deep voice taking a husky tone. Erin knew her eyes widened when he held up his hands in mock surrender. "Only if you promise to keep your hands off me, that is. I am no easy score."

Erin smiled widely. "Oh I don't know. I can't promise not to ravish you." Her heart accelerated at the thought of being alone with him in her bed.

"Come on. We can talk until you fall asleep." He held out a hand and she took it.

It was uncanny how comfortable she felt with Padriag. It was as if they'd known each other for years, felt a sense of belonging in each other's lives. When she considered that once he was free, she'd not be part of his life, it saddened her. Although, she suspected, he would remain in touch in gratitude if she'd helped him.

"This way." She walked to her bedroom which was opposite Audrey's.

Once in the bedroom, Erin climbed onto the bed and slid under the blankets feeling like a virgin bride. Padriag lay atop the blankets, pulling the throw from the foot of the bed over himself.

"Bed's pretty comfortable," he said sliding his hands under his head and staring up at the ceiling. "Things are changing," he began. "Liam and I are being kicked out of Esland, by the prince."

"Why?" Erin looked to him and couldn't help but admire his profile. The man was stunning, from the square jawline to his lips and his perfectly shaped nose. She wondered how many women he'd seduced during his time there. Probably never had to actually do much pursuing.

"Apparently we broke their laws by leaving the realm. It's

strictly forbidden. The first time he gave us a warning, stating that we couldn't leave again."

Turning on her side to face him, Erin said, "So being here, you violated the laws of that land and have to leave."

He looked at her. "We plan to leave once the prince, and his army returned. They went off somewhere, of course being newcomers, nothing was shared with us about where or why."

"Where will you go? I thought the place you lived is not safe."

Padriag closed his eyes. "Meliot can't kill us. He can make us wish for death, but for some reason we cannot die there. We can ask Prince Sterling's sisters, who rule over the realm called Atlandia, to give us asylum. To be honest, I would prefer to live in a cabin in the woods rather than have to serve a royal."

Of course Padriag was exhausted, Erin considered. For centuries he and the other four men had battled, been held captive, tortured, and suffered at the hands of Meliot. Most men would break at this point. The fact that Padriag kept his sense of humor was commendable.

It was in all probability a defense mechanism, but it seemed to work for him, kept him sane all those years.

Erin cupped his jaw, turning him to face her again. "Don't give up hope. It breaks my heart to think of you there alone and without it."

When he brushed a tear from her face, she was surprised. Hadn't been aware the thought of him alone and hopeless had brought her to tears.

"I am not sure I can. To be honest with you, there are days I just want to go to sleep and not wake."

"Padriag! No." Erin slid closer and pressed her forehead to his cheek. "Please don't. Things will work out. I will have enough hope for both of us and promise to not give up until you are free."

He touched her face, the touch light as air. "Thank you."

When his mouth came over hers, she sagged with relief. The feel of his lips pressed on hers was what she'd wanted since he'd appeared. Except now she wanted more, she wanted him. Needed to make love to him, to physically express herself.

The desire rose, flaming the soft embers of passion that she'd thought to have sealed away. But the kiss, one kiss from Padriag and Erin's entire world changed. They were meant to be. He was the one, her other half, the one thing that had been missing from her life.

Their tongues danced, the movements primal, each one communicating to the other the growing need.

Erin broke the kiss, her breathing harsh to her own ears. "I want to be with you Padriag. I need you."

Instead of a reply, Padriag took her mouth again, pulling her closer, one hand respectfully at the center of her back, the other cupping her head.

Clinging to him as he ravaged her mouth, his tongue then sliding down the side of her neck and back up to her ear. His breath brought chills of excitement.

"Not like this," he whispered. "I want you more than you know. Think about you all the time. But to be with you, as much as I want to, would make being away that much harder."

Pulling her against his chest, he let out a shaky breath. Beneath her ear, the thundering of his heart and harsh breaths were an unmistakable sign that he was as aroused as she.

Erin reached up and stroked his hair. "I understand. But know that I think of you often as well. I don't know how, it seems so soon, but you've already a piece of my heart."

A soft chuckle rumbled in his chest. "You are special to me as well. Now, sleep," Padriag replied. "I have a feeling the next days will take a lot of energy."

For a long while, she listened to the lull of his breathing and steady heartbeat. Lying next to him, being held in his embrace, was not only thrilling, but comforting. For the first time since leaving Evalyn's house, she felt safe and secure. Padriag was her shelter from the ravages of a storm.

Chapter Ten

A fully dressed and made-up Aubrey sat at the kitchen island with a cup of coffee in her hand. Her eyes widened when both Erin and Padriag entered the kitchen the following morning. "Did you two kids sleep well? Sleep at all?"

A warm heat traveled up Erin's neck to her face. "We talked and slept, that is all."

Gaze traveling up Padriag's bare legs, Aubrey sipped from her cup. "Right."

"Do you have any clothes that would fit me?" Padriag asked, not seeming to mind either Aubrey's insinuations or her perusal.

"If my clothes fit you, I will kill myself," Aubrey replied. "How dare you, sir."

"I told you," Erin said. "You will have to wait until we get to Dunimarle." She poured two cups of coffee from the pot Aubrey had prepared, added cream and gave Padriag a questioning look. "Sugar?"

"You can call me that if you wish, I prefer 'babe,'" the smug man replied.

Narrowing her eyes playfully, Erin plopped the cup in front of him and walked to the other side of the kitchen island and climbed up onto a stool.

"What is the plan for today?" Aubrey said. "Go to the castle, tell the others what happened and then what?"

Erin sipped her coffee and replied. "I got up after you fell asleep. Thoughts and words kept shooting through my mind. I wasn't even trying to think of a spell. When the same words wouldn't stop coming to me, I began writing them down. Most of it is a jumbled mess that doesn't make any sense." She glanced at Padriag who listened with interest. "Maybe some of it can be part of your spell."

He nodded. "After Meliot's appearance it makes me wonder what is meant to help and what comes only to send us down rabbit trails."

Having showered that morning before putting the same tunic back on, Padriag's hair was damp. Red waves clung together, one falling over his brow. He pushed it away only for it to fall back. The man was every woman's fantasy, as evident by not only her inability to keep from looking at him, but also the constant glances Aubrey slid at him when she thought Erin wasn't looking. Not that she blamed her cousin one bit. The tunic clung to every hard surface of his body, accentuating the thick arms, wide shoulders, and broad, muscular chest.

"I-I best shower and change, then we can go," Erin said, sliding from her seat. "Won't be long."

"That's true," Aubrey said as she walked away. "Erin is

the only woman I know who can be ready in fifteen minutes and look as if she spent hours primping."

Erin smiled at her cousin. "I'm sure you don't mind keeping Padriag company."

Her cousin grinned and turned to Padraig. "Not at all. Tell me about your life here in Scotland before you got abducted. I'm super curious to know what life was really like back then."

THE ATMOSPHERE CRACKLED with apprehension on the drive to the castle, a silent urgency filling the air. A sense that something was about to happen made Erin's pulse pound in her ears as she gripped the steering wheel. Every few seconds, she forced herself to loosen her grip, to lower her shoulders, but the tight coil of unease in her stomach refused to unwind.

Beside her, Padraig stared out the window, eyes locked on the countryside that blurred past. She wondered what he saw —not just the passing scenery, but the glimmers of centuries gone by. How many times had he watched the world shift and evolve? Rulers rising and falling, wars starting and ending, cultures transforming beyond recognition. The secrets he carried, the truths that had been warped by history books, could rewrite everything scholars thought to be true.

If nothing else, she hoped one day he would put it all into words. Even if no one believed him, his account would be the only firsthand experiences of a world long lost.

"Look!" Aubrey's voice cut through the thick silence,

sharp with alarm. She pointed to the left. "That's ... not normal."

Erin's gaze snapped toward where the castle should have come into view, her breath catching. They had just passed through Culross, the last village before the castle. But where the ancient stronghold should have been, perched on its usual rise, there was nothing but an impenetrable wall of swirling mist.

Her foot eased off the gas. "What the hell?" she breathed. "Is that ... fog?"

The mist wasn't natural. It coiled thick and dense, a solid, shifting mass that seemed to swallow the castle whole. It was so solid that no outline of turrets or stone walls were visible.

"Damn it," Padraig muttered, his entire body tensing. "Pull over. Now. Someone call the castle. I need to know if they can see it from the other side."

Erin fumbled for her phone, her fingers clumsy as she put the call on speaker. The first ring had barely finished when Gwen answered, her voice taut with worry.

"Erin. I was just about to call you. Don't try to come here."

Padraig stared at the phone. "Do you see the mists?"

"Yes, it's like a wall surrounding us," Gwen replied, her breath uneven. "We tried to drive through it, but it's impossible to see once you enter it. We were afraid to go any farther —might hit a tree or ... something."

A cold shiver slithered up Erin's spine, goosebumps formed on her arms. The world she thought she understood was unraveling.

"We're on the other side," she murmured, gripping the phone tighter. "The castle's not visible from here."

Padraig's eyes were sharp, unreadable as he studied the view.

A deep voice crackled through the speaker. It was Tristan. "Padraig? Can you get through?"

Padraig didn't answer right away. His gaze stayed locked on the unnatural mist. Then, finally, with lack of certainty, he said, "Probably."

Gwen's voice came back, laced with apprehension. "Call us back if you can't make it." The call ended.

For a long moment, Padraig sat motionless, head cocked to the side then upright, he studied the swirling fog. Then he exhaled, turned to Erin, and spoke, his tone serious.

"Be ready. The moment you see an opening, drive straight through. Do not stop. Do you understand?"

Erin nodded. "Yes."

A grin spread across his face. "Good." Pushing the car door open, he climbed and began walking toward the mist.

"What the hell is he doing?" Aubrey breathed, leaning between the seats, her face pale.

They could only watch, hearts pounding, as Padraig strode toward the mist—barefoot, clad only in a loose tunic that barely reached mid-thigh. Despite his lack of attire, the purposeful long strides and set of wide shoulders exuded power, command of the situation.

And then—he lifted his arms.

Aubrey sucked in a sharp breath.

"Holy hell."

Erin's mouth went dry at the sight before her. Dim

morning sunlight seeped through the cloudy sky and cast just the right illumination to highlight every taut muscle, every shift of sinew beneath his golden skin—and the firm curve of his very bare backside.

Aubrey exhaled slowly. "Damn," she whispered, reverent. "That is one amazing view."

"Yep," was all Erin could manage as a reply.

Something like electrical blue and gold sparks erupted in Padraig's palms, flickering as if alive. He moved his hands in slow, deliberate arcs, sweeping them downward until they hovered at shoulder level. The circular fiery rings grew, stretching out like ravenous tongues toward the mist.

Erin clenched the steering wheel, her fingers trembling.

Then he walked forward, and the mist swallowed him, and he seemed to vanish, except for the flames that shined through the thick hovering void.

Seconds ticked by, agonizingly slow.

A violent explosion of color detonated through the fog, streaks of blue, gold, and violet cutting through the mist. A tunnel of raw, crackling energy stretched open, pulsating with twisting currents of power.

Aubrey gasped. "What the actual hell?"

A deafening, high-pitched screech sent Erin's senses reeling. Like microphone feedback turned up to an unbearable volume, it stabbed through her skull, making her wince.

The tunnel wavered. The screeching grew.

Aubrey grabbed her arm. "Go!"

Erin snapped into action. She slammed the gas pedal. The car lurched forward, gears grinding as she shoved it into second, then third, then fourth.

The tunnel was both terrifying and breathtaking—a swirling, living storm of energy, twisting and weaving like a cosmic dance. Colors she couldn't name slashed through the air, warping and shifting, forming impossible patterns.

She wanted to stare. To take it in.

But the walls of the tunnel moved closer.

"Oh my god, it's closing," Aubrey yelled. "Go faster."

"Don't have to tell me twice," Erin pushed her car to the limit and raced forward until coming to a screeching stop when emerging on the other side. Dunimarle stood before them, whole and untouched.

Three couples, Gwen and Tristan, Niall and Tammie and Sabrina and Gavin, were grouped together.

With the car still rocking from the abrupt stop, Erin threw open the door and ran straight for the collapsing tunnel.

"Padriag!"

Strong arms caught her before she could get anywhere near the mists and lights, lifting her off the ground as easily as if she weighed nothing.

"You cannot go any closer. You will be injured. Padriag is unharmed."

The deep, familiar voice caught her by surprise.

It was Niall MacTavish.

She fought against his grip, twisting violently. "How do you know?"

Niall's grip tightened. "We have been recipients of Padraig's power." His voice was steady "It was quite unpleasant."

The tunnel convulsed. Its energy spiraled inward, collapsing in on itself until nothing remained but the mist.

A shadow emerged.

Electric tendrils still crackled around him, flickering against the night. Padraig stumbled forward, the last of the lightening that surrounded him fading, his steps unsteady.

Erin sagged with relief.

The tunic, looked to be singed on the hem and edges of the sleeves. His face was covered in soot and hair stood on end. Still, Padriag managed a wide grin and held his arms out as if preparing to take flight. "Am I superhero material or what?"

His knees buckled, body sagged, and then he flopped, face-first, into the grass.

"Or what," Niall muttered, striding forward as the other two men rushed to Padraig's side.

Erin took a step forward, but a hand on her arm held her back.

"Come inside, we'll see to him there," Gwen said. "Tristan said he could pass out. Apparently, when he expends that much energy, it depletes him, but it doesn't last long."

The men hurried past carrying Padriag and they followed.

Just before entering, she looked over her shoulder. The mists were evaporating, slowly fading until all evidence of it was gone.

Chapter Eleven

After a hot shower—one of the things he missed the most when not in Scotland—Padriag felt renewed. Glad to be fully clothed and with shoes on his feet, he strode from the bedroom he'd woken up in and hurried to find the others. There wasn't any time to waste, they had to figure out what happened before he felt the pull to return to Esland.

Once on the first floor, he followed the sound of voices into the dining room. Everyone surrounded the table and was eating when he walked in. They looked up.

Erin's gaze swept over him, which affected him as much as if she touched him where her eyes roamed.

"Join us," Gwen said, "Discuss while we eat."

The chair next to Erin had been left empty, so he pulled it back and lowered to sit. "Where are Sabrina and Gavin?"

Tristan replied, "He accompanied her to work, in London."

"It couldn't be put off. As much as they hate not to be

here to help," Tammie added. "Gavin will be returning in a couple days. In case he is needed."

The fact that the pair was doing something besides trying to save him was gratifying. "I am glad. All of you should be living your life instead of putting things off because of me."

"It will be a battle. You are aware we will never give up, so stop bringing it up," Liam said walking in and giving Padriag a pointed look. "You could have left a note when you left Esland."

Padriag returned the look. "I was asleep. Then next thing I know I'm in a strange kitchen wearing one piece of clothing ..." He frowned. "What do you mean by a battle?"

Taking his time, Liam pulled a chair and sat next to Erin's cousin, Aubrey, who studied him as if he were a work of art. The Brit was attractive, Padriag supposed.

After leisurely buttering a piece of bread, Liam met his gaze. "All I know is that the path to freedom will be hard fought, my friend."

"Meliot has gained some of his powers back. He is affecting things here," Tristan stated. "What we cannot understand is how."

"Davina's death released her powers into the realm and, of course, since they were dark powers, Meliot must have acquired them," Liam said, his tone somber.

Tammie blew out a breath. "Is that why it will be hard to free Padriag?"

Liam nodded. "Yes. Then there is the matter of finding a home. We cannot remain in Esland much longer."

"What about a spell?" Liam asked.

Erin slid a notebook from beside her plate. "We have been working on it while Padriag ... er slept."

"You slept?" Liam frowned at Padriag and looked to Tristan. "Why did you let him sleep? He has work to do."

"I had to use magic."

Liam nodded again, understanding what had occurred. "Let me see." He read over whatever was on Erin's notebook.

"I think we should try it," Gwen said, sliding a look to him. Padriag was almost positive it wouldn't work. Not after what Liam had stated. There were more the Brit wasn't saying. When Liam left details out, it wasn't an indication anything good was to come.

"I agree," Tammie said. "If nothing else, we will get a sense if we're on the right path with what we've come up with."

When he turned to look at Erin, it was obvious by her pinched expression that she was as unsure as he was. Despite knowing everyone around the table was serious about saving him, Padriag wanted nothing more than to enjoy the meal and spend time with his friends. Too soon it would be harder and harder to return to Scotland. He was weak, though he did his best to hide it. The magic he'd used to cut through the fog had taken a toll on him.

Erin cleared her throat and looked down at the words she'd written. "Here we go."

Everyone was solemn, Gwen and Tammie held hands and closed their eyes.

"By love unbroken, by bond unshaken,
I summon the heart that fate has taken.

By moon's soft glow and sun's first light,
Break these chains, undo the night.
Through endless time, through veil and mist,
Let not our bond be lost, dismissed.
By whispered vow and promise sworn,
Return, this knight, from where he was torn.
From shadows deep and silent grave,
Rise once more, be strong and brave.
By fate's design and heart's decree,
The knight's return will come to be."

An expectant heavy silence hung in the air, each person seeming reluctant to break whatever, if anything, happened from the spell.

Noting tears sliding down Erin's face, Padriag took her hand in his.

All of a sudden something traveled through him, a spark of sorts. The hairs on his arms stood on end and there was a slight tingling at his nape. Whatever it was must have affected the others because everyone was looking at their arms. Still no one spoke as if not wishing to scare away whatever would happen next.

The lights in the room brightened and dimmed, then flashed before they went out, leaving the room lit only from the light from the corridor.

Tiny sparks of light floated in the air, twirling and flitting about like fireflies. Like stars in the sky, there had to be thousands of them.

Then, what looked to be something like a ribbon of light formed as the lights joined into long streamers and continued their odd motions, twisting in the air, circling over their heads.

His skin tingled, goosebumps formed on every inch of his body, it wasn't unpleasant, but more as if warmth filled him. When everyone turned to look at Padriag, he lifted his arms noting that the little lights covered his skin.

A strange surge of energy shot through his body, and he jerked back onto the chair, barely hearing the exclamations of surprise from the others.

Then, just as gently as the lights came, they floated upward and vanished.

"Are you alright?" Erin asked, her hand pressed to his upper chest. "Can you talk? Breathe?"

Padriag nodded, although honestly not sure how he felt.

Pushing back from the table, he stood, feeling strong and renewed.

"I think whatever that was gave me strength. I feel great."

Liam's lips curved. "You are ready to face all that will come your way."

Giving his friend a droll look, Padriag crossed his arms. "Look Obi One, stop talking in riddles. Just tell me the truth. That Meliot is about to unleash holy hell on me."

Tristan and Niall looked between him and Liam. Tristan let out a huff. "Liam, what do you know?"

"Nothing more. Like I said, he will face trials, and his release will be harder fought than any of ours."

Tammie gave Liam an exasperated look. "Can you at least give specifics of what he needs to prepare for?"

"I will speak to Padriag alone. What I have to say is only for him to hear," Liam replied.

The familiar tug from the alter-world urged his return. "Let's talk, then," Padriag remarked. "But I want Tristan and Niall to be present."

He slid a look to Erin. "I expect them to fill you in on whatever they deem pertinent."

Tears sprang to her eyes, and she gave him a shaky smile. Even with a reddened nose and shiny eyes, Erin was beautiful. He wanted nothing more than to take her into his arms and hold her. He prayed to have the opportunity before having to leave.

The four men went into the library and settled into comfortable chairs after Tristan closed the doors.

By Liam's expression, it was obvious what he would impart was not good news. Padriag stood, uncorked a crystal decanter and poured whiskey into a glass, downed it and then served himself another two fingers.

When he sat down, Liam spoke again. "Not everything I saw is exact. However, as we have learned my visions always come to be."

"I don't want to know. Not now." Padriag's voice shook with emotion.

Just as Liam started to speak, Padriag jumped to his feet and stormed from the room, down the short hallway and out the front door. He kept walking without a destination in mind, unseeing past the sudden blurriness. Tears of frustration slid down his face and he made no effort to brush them away.

Despite the renewed strength coursing through him, Padriag was bone-deep weary. Not just tired in body but hollowed out in spirit.

Somewhere along the way, he'd lost the will to continue fighting. He collapsed onto the grass, letting gravity take over, his back pressing into the earth as if hoping it might absorb some of the ache lodged inside him.

Above him, the sky stretched vast and endless, a tapestry of blue streaked with clouds so soft and white they barely looked real. They floated lazily, like they had all the time in the world. A cruel contrast to the relentless pressure building inside him. The beauty of it struck something raw. There were no skies like this in the other world. No scent of moss, or the subtle, grounding blend of sun-warmed soil and wind-whipped grass.

That world felt sterile. Harsh. Hollow.

But here ... here was Scotland. And in this fleeting moment, it was the only place in the world he wanted to be. The sounds, smells of moss and pine with just a hint of salty sea, soothed his weary soul. Reminded him of who he was before everything had fallen apart. He clung to that sense of belonging like a man drowning clings to a raft.

"It's a beautiful day," Erin said softly, sinking down to lie beside him with deep breaths that hinted she'd run to catch up. Her breath was quick, chest rising and falling, but her presence was a balm. Quiet. Steady.

She reached for his hand, threading her fingers through his without another word. And thank God for that, because if she'd said anything more, he might've broken and, worse than tears, he feared he might actually sob. So he stayed still, letting her warmth seep into him, breathing in the scent of earth and her and peace.

Minutes passed, how long he didn't know. Time somehow seemed to soften around them.

Then, with a tenderness that struck deep, Erin nestled against his side, her voice soft, gentle. "I cannot imagine what you're feeling. What you and the others have endured is beyond cruel. It's not fair. None of it is. And no one blames you for wanting to stop fighting. You must be so very tired."

He nodded, a slight jerk of his chin. Tired wasn't even the word. He was wrecked. Drained. And fed up with Meliot's twisted games. Every time he thought he could rest, something else ripped peace away.

When Erin pressed her lips to his jaw, his eyes fluttered shut. God, it had been torture not to reach for her last night. Pure willpower had kept him from crossing the line, from taking what his heart had long since claimed. But now, with her hand in his and her lips on his skin, the ache in him deepened. If they had made love, he knew—he *knew*—he would be lost without her.

Her voice came again, quiet but unwavering, threading through the chaos in his soul like a lifeline.

"Just one more fight, Padriag. Not for anyone else but for *you*. For your freedom. Dig down deep. Find whatever's left and help us."

If only it were that simple. If promises alone could carry him through. His body might just have enough left in it. But his heart? His spirit? He wasn't so sure.

"I don't know," he rasped. "I don't know if I can."

She turned his face to hers with gentle fingers, her eyes, those green, expressive long-lashed eyes, piercing straight through his defenses.

"You can," she said, fierce in her softness. "I know you can."

And in that moment, words were useless. He reached for her, covering her mouth with his in a kiss that was both surrender and plea. She tasted like hope and something sweeter than mercy. Her arms wrapped around his neck, drawing him closer, her kiss full of fire and devotion. She didn't need to say another word, he felt it all in the way she held him. She'd fight for him. She already was.

Padriag crushed her against him, needing the warmth of her, the weight of her, the realness. The scent of her hair, the softness of her skin, he soaked it in, desperate for the reminder that life still held something beautiful.

"Fight for me," she whispered, lips brushing his ear, her breath sending a shiver through him.

Damn if she didn't make him feel like he mattered. Like he was still the hero of his own story.

"I will," he whispered back, though the words came hollow and unsure. He wanted to believe them. Needed to. But truthfully, Padriag wasn't sure if he could.

Maybe, just maybe, he'd find a way.

It was strange to have a woman's hand in his, but holding Erin's was like having an anchor that kept him from floating away.

They walked into the house. No one was in sight. The women had gone, to allow the men privacy.

"Go," Erin whispered, rising up on her toes to kiss his cheek.

When she released his hand, Padriag took a deep breath and walked into the library and saw that Gavin had joined Tristan, Niall and Liam.

The Brit gave him a bored look. "Now let's get on with this. Padriag and I have to return immediately."

"What exactly did you see?" Tristan's voice was low, tense, his gaze sweeping the room like a man searching for threats in every shadow. "If something's coming, we need to be ready."

Liam didn't answer right away. His eyes like still, icy water, the weight of what he carried evident in the set of his jaw. "It's going to take all five of us," he said finally. "Every single one. No exceptions."

The room stilled. A cold dread spreading like smoke.

Padriag's stomach turned to stone. Whatever Liam had seen was unimaginable. His mind whirled in anticipation.

Liam took a breath, and when he spoke again, his voice was quieter but heavier. "This is the last quest. We will all return to the other realm. And if we fail ... we don't come back."

Silence fell like a blade.

No one moved. No one spoke. They just sat, still as stone, as if moving might make Liam's words real.

Padriag stood, fists clenched. "No. I won't allow this. Not after what you've all been through. You earned your freedom, you can't be dragged back into that place."

Liam met his eyes, and despite the gravity of the moment, there was a strange warmth in his smile. "It's not about what we want, Padriag. It's happening, whether we're ready or not."

"Good," Niall said, breaking the tension with a steel edge in his voice. "Then we go. Together we are stronger and this time we won't fail."

Liam nodded once. "You'll each need a weapon. Keep it close. I don't know if you will be given any time before you are compelled back."

Gavin raised an eyebrow. "Can I bring a gun? Better yet, a machine gun?"

"They won't work," Tristan said grimly. "Not in that place."

"Not against dark magic," Liam confirmed. "Steel, fire, skill—that's what we'll need."

Padriag sagged. As if the warlock hadn't already brought them centuries of penance, now, once again. They'd have to beat a quest to win their freedom. If it was at all possible.

Tristan stood, already half-turned toward the door. "I'm going to find Gwen. If we're being pulled back ... I need to spend as much time as possible with her."

He paused, looking back at the others. "You should do the same. We may not get another opportunity."

Chapter Twelve

Needing to see about the yoga studio, Aubrey had left making Erin promise to be careful and not go anywhere alone.

Erin joined the rest of the women around a table in the conservatory, the glass walls making it seem as if they were outdoors while protecting them from the now falling drizzle. Although cloudy, the view of the garden and the plush green hills with sprinkles of lavender in the distance was enchanting.

"I have a horrible feeling about what Liam is telling them," Gwen said, sliding a look in the direction of the library. "They have been in there a long time."

Erin frowned. "Padriag mentioned that he was already feeling the pull to return, I imagine they will continue speaking until he leaves." A part of her ached at not seeing him once again before he returned to the alter-world, the feel of his kisses still forefront on her mind. She wished for at least one more.

What if he didn't return? How would she be able to continue everyday life knowing he was trapped forever? Her chest tightened just thinking about it. They had to free him, otherwise she'd not be able to live with herself.

Tristan, Gavin and Niall entered the room, their grim expressions and paleness revealing that whatever they'd been told had not been good.

"Liam has gone to see John," Niall explained. "We need to speak to each of you."

Each man took their partner by the hand, avoiding eye contact with Erin as they guided them from the room.

Erin's heart sank. Padriag must have returned to the alterworld as he had not entered with the others. She closed her eyes and leaned back, willing her body to relax if just for a moment. Soon she'd find out what was to happen next, and since she was now sure it would be bad news, perhaps this would be the last time she'd be able to clear her mind.

Erin stood and went closer to the window. A whispered plea formed in her mind as she looked up to the sky. "I need to know the reason why I am here," she said to no one in particular. "Show me the reason."

She was not sure what she'd hoped for, perhaps a booming voice from the sky or a bolt of lightning hitting her and filling her with superpowers. The silence, although disappointing, was not a surprise.

"Erin." Padriag's voice was startling. Erin whirled to see him standing just inside the door.

"I thought you'd left." She rushed to him. "I know whatever Liam said wasn't good news. Can you tell me what he said?"

Unable to keep from it, she reached for his hand. "Padriag?"

"You asked that I fight for you. For us," Padriag began. "Give me the strength because I am not sure I have enough right now. I have to regain not only mental and physical strength, but more than ever, I need my powers to be renewed for what's ahead."

How was she supposed to help with that? Erin was sure she was powerless. Unlike the others, she'd never been exposed to any kind of magic, witchcraft, or any mystical crafts. The only thing she could do was to rely on reasoning. There had to be a reason she'd been chosen to help Padriag, and a reason Meliot had captured her and taken her to the other realm.

"I have no answer as to what the reason is for me being part of this, but know I will do what I can."

"Whatever the reason," Padriag said, wrapping his arms around Erin's waist. "I am glad."

Erin leaned in, her head coming to rest on his shoulder. "I am glad too, but I want to be helpful. I need to do whatever is necessary."

Something like an electrical shock made her gasp. "What was that?"

"What?" Padriag asked with a puzzled expression. "What happened."

Another jolt struck, this one so strong the hairs on her arms stood on end. Holding her arms up, she gaped at them. "It's like I'm being shocked. Ouch!" she cried out when another one passed through her.

Padriag pulled her against his body, holding her close. "I don't see anything."

The last jolt was so strong, Erin gritted her teeth and groaned. "What the hell?"

For the next few moments they waited in silence, Erin braced in case it happened again.

"I think they stopped." She blew out a breath. "What was that?"

"I am not sure." Padriag studied her. "Do you feel different?"

At first she took a tentative step away from the safety of his embrace and then another, she walked in a circle. Something like an undercurrent sizzled beneath her skin, it wasn't uncomfortable, but definitely unsettling.

She met Padriag's gaze. There he stood, a weary warrior, and yet strength and power emanated from him. Deep in her soul, she knew he would fight until the last breath and not give up no matter how tired he was.

How was it possible to feel so strongly for someone in such a short amount of time? Their future was unstable, whether he returned or not. At the same time, there was no doubt in her mind that the man who stood before her was to be joined to her for the rest of their life.

Something totally different surged within. A desperate longing, an overwhelming need consumed every inch of her body.

"I ... I need you to come with me." Grabbing his hand, she pulled him from the room, up the stairs and into the bedroom where she was to stay.

Padriag looked around and then at her, his Adam's apple moved as he swallowed.

"We are going to make love," Erin said, with more assuredness than she felt.

There was something like relief on his face, his gaze locking with hers. Then closing the distance, he took her into his arms, mouth over hers, hands sliding down and up her back as he ravished her lips.

She clawed at his clothes, glad when he helped by pulling the tunic up over his head.

His muscles were rippling, each peak and valley demanding attention. One day she'd be able to pay every inch homage. But in this moment, there was a crucial need that sizzled under her skin and needed to be satiated.

"We have to hurry," Erin said, her urgent tone husky almost as if someone else spoke through her.

Between kisses, they undressed until fully bare. Padriag lifted her easily and carried her to the bed. There was hunger in his darkened gaze, as they fell onto the bed.

"You are so damn perfect," his husky voice sent tingles across her skin.

Erin could barely keep from yanking the man over her. Urgency filled every fiber of her being. Something was going to happen, something had to happen.

Seeming to sense what she was feeling, Padriag covered her body with his own. "I have to do this quickly. The pull back to the alter-world is strengthening. I am so sorry."

Erin was at the point of writhing. "Yes, hurry."

He began shaking, as if shivering from the cold. Erin wasn't sure if it was because it was the first time in so long or because he was fighting to remain there. When Padriag lifted his hips, Erin reached between them and wrapped her fingers around his generous shaft. Definitely gifted in that department. It was too bad they'd not get to linger.

Both let out a groan as Padriag thrust into her, his girth stretching and length filling her. Erin threw her head back as he began moving, sliding in and out of her, each movement a relief to her overheated body.

"Erin," he moaned into her ear, the heat of his breath erotic.

"So good," she replied, lifting her hips to meet each plunge. "Oh!"

"Faster," Erin said wrapping her arms around his shoulders.

Suddenly the room went dark.

Padriag didn't seem to notice, or if he did, it didn't stop him from continuing forward. His body in rhythm with hers. Their lovemaking reaching the crescendo their movements became faster and harder. On the brink, Erin threw her head back and let out a stifled cry as every part of her being broke apart into a million pieces.

As a second wave of release washed over her, she clung to Padriag, her body trembling, her vision a blur of lights.

His husky moan rolled over her, a tidal wave of pleasure taking them both. He shuddered and buried his face in her hair as he became lost in his own release.

For a few precious moments, they remained joined, his body sprawled over her as she ran her hands up and down his back.

Moments later, rolling to his side, Padriag pulled her into

his arms. He pressed kisses in a path from her mouth, across to her jawline and then dragged his tongue down the side of Erin's neck.

Erin shivered with delight her eyes falling shut. She could spend days like this, basking in the afterglow of making love with him.

"I have to go," Padriag whispered, kissing her on the lips.

"Promise me you will come back to me," Erin replied, doing her best to blink tears away. "I mean it, Padriag. You have to."

His lips curved. "I will do what I can."

A hand on both sides of his face, Erin studied him for a long moment. "You are the bravest man I've ever met."

Warmth filled his gaze. "There is so much I want to say to you. I wish we had more time."

"We will. Once this is over." Erin brushed an errant lock from his brow wanting to memorize every part of his face. "When you return."

When Padriag materialized in the alter-world, the first thing he did was ensure he was dressed. He'd been nude when the pull became too strong to fight, and he'd jumped from the bed to yank on his pants. Barefoot and shirtless, he was glad that at least his bottom half was covered.

The surroundings were strange, the dim room lit only by the fires from hammered metal sconces and a black iron candelabrum atop a rustic wooden table.

Padriag swiveled, turning in a circle to take in the space.

He seemed to be in a log cottage. Other than the sounds of his breathing, the place was eerily silent.

Across the room was a coat of arms. Atop a red background, a golden lion standing on its hind legs, holding a sword in one paw and seven arrows in the other. While keeping alert, Padriag studied the floor, testing each plank before taking steps toward the shield. He stopped and listened intently to make sure nothing, or no one, made their way there.

When satisfied to being alone, he neared the wall and looked up at the coat of arms with two swords crossed at the blade under it.

"Janssen. Interesting."

Why was there a Dutch coat of arms there? Was there another person also trapped, or perhaps had been saved?

Before reaching for one of the swords, he assessed every detail, from the hook on which the swords were hung on, to the bricks behind. Then slowly, he took a sword down and shifted it in his hand. The weapon was of a good weight for him, the blade sharp. It had been forged well. The craftsmanship on the handle was obviously the work of an excellent blacksmith.

Sword in hand, Padriag turned in a full circle, once again ensuring he was alone. A crackling noise got his attention and, holding the sword with both hands in front of him, he crept through an archway to the next room.

This area was a sitting room of sorts. There were several chairs in front of a large fireplace, arms and backs carved with designs. Pelts were strewn over the chairs for extra warmth, although the fire that burned brightly emanated enough to warm the room.

Someone had been there recently, since there was a fire. Once again testing the flooring, he moved to a window, opened a shutter with one hand and peered out.

No doubt about it, he was back in the alter-world. The purple sky with yellowish plumes crisscrossing was lit by two moons. The ground looked to be frozen, banks of snow forming around the thick trunks of twisted trees.

It was the first time he'd seen golden trees with pinkish leaves. The trunks were twisted as if formed by a child given free rein with clay. Long tentacle-like roots grew out of the ground, the ends reaching upward.

Padriag frowned, scanning the ground for footprints until noticing the edge of another building to the far right, most of it behind the house. It looked to be a barn.

Unsure of what could be out there, and the setting suns, he decided it was best to wait and leave further exploring until the morning. He walked back to the first room, noting there was food and drink on a sideboard.

As hungry and thirsty as he was, it was best not to take a chance.

The air shifted, and Padriag planted his feet wide, raising his sword in ready defiance.

"Why are you half dressed?" Liam asked emerging from a doorway, a sword held before him.

"Why are you so damn ugly?" Padriag retorted.

Liam lowered his sword, knowing it had to be the real Padriag by the comment. "Where the hell are we?"

"Some Dutch guy's cabin," Padriag replied motioning to

the coat of arms with his head. "He, or someone, has been here recently, there's a fire in the other room."

Liam eyed the food. "You didn't eat anything did you?"

Instead of a reply, he gave the Brit a droll look.

"I suppose we wait."

They went to the front room. While Liam looked out the same window Padriag had earlier, Padriag got closer to the fireplace to warm his feet and torso. Then he took a pelt and threw it over his shoulders.

"We'll take turns sleeping," Liam said turning from the window. "Where are your clothes?"

"I decided to become a nudist," Padriag snapped. "Obviously my clothes are in the other realm."

Liam's eyebrows shot upward. "Oh." He turned back to the window. "Someone is coming. It's Veylen."

Moments later, the door opened and Veylen walked in, snow falling from his fur-lined cape landing on the wooden floor and melting into small puddles.

"The Prince asked that I bring you two mounts. The aurochs are in the stable. I've ensured enough food and water that should last through the winter."

After exchanging confused looks with Liam, Padriag met the Eslander's gaze. "Who's home is this? Is anyone else staying here?"

"A friend of Prince Sterling. He is called Janssen. The owner has been unable to utilize this home for a long time." Veylen glanced past them to the room where Padriag had materialized. "I suggest rationing the food if you hope to get through the freeze. You can go out hunting I suppose."

The warrior turned to leave.

"Wait," Liam said moving closer to Veylen. "Why did the Sterling have us come here?"

"You require shelter and food. People from your realm are ill-prepared for this one. You may live here as long as you wish."

Padriag cocked his head to the side. "We managed to survive in this realm for three hundred years. I think we've got this."

"Mmm," Veylen replied, his gaze moving from Padriag's bare feet to his unclothed torso. "That is good to know." With that he left.

"Hopefully there are shoes and clothes here somewhere," Liam said, moving toward a corridor that led toward the back of the home.

There were three adequately sized bedchambers, each with a bed, trunk, and basin stand. In the trunks were clothes and shoes, which Padriag went through until finding a tunic, socks and boots that fit.

"This is interesting," Liam said leaning against the door jamb. "I would like to know what happened to Janssen. He may have died."

"Or he went to Esland, and they don't let him leave," Padriag remarked.

"There is that"

THAT EVENING, they ate a simple meal of apples, bread and cheese, washed down with a surprisingly good wine. Padriag could barely keep his eyes open, and he wondered how long it had been since he slept. Time moved so differently when traveling between the realms, yet judging by the way he felt, it could have been twenty-four hours or more.

"I am going back to the other realm. I promised John to stay for a few days." Liam seemed troubled. "Nothing feels certain, but I haven't had any visions, which I take as a good sign."

All Padriag wanted was to climb into bed and go to sleep. "I will be safe here. You do not have to keep coming. Please go Liam. John has been patient, and I appreciate it, but he deserves time with you."

SEVEN DAYS PASSED and although things were way too quiet, Padriag had to admit he was enjoying life at the log cabin in the middle of a forest with only aurochs for company. The beasts seemed friendly enough when he wandered into the stable to open the doors and allow them out to roam inside the corral. They stayed within the closed area, despite the fact it would be child's play for them to break free.

He decided the animals were a gentle sort, unless perhaps aggravated by someone with a death wish.

As the last sun began its descent, he went inside to check on a pot of stew he was preparing. Potatoes and carrots floated in the bubbling broth. The aroma of the spicy meal wafting through the kitchen. He dipped a large spoon into the liquid, and he brought it up to his lips to blow on it. Then he tasted.

Moments later, he pushed an empty bowl away, deciding that two servings were more than enough.

After washing the dishes, he took the pot with the rest of the stew to store it in an outside pantry.

To keep food cold, a small doorless room had been attached just outside the kitchen where the frigid outdoor temperatures would keep food from spoilage. Inside were shelves on which jars and wrapped bundles were placed.

Once that was done, Padriag went to the adjacent room to sit before the fire. Eyes focused on the wavering flames, his mind drifted to Erin. Every day since returning to the alterworld he went over every detail of being with Erin. From waking up next to her to getting through the mists. Finally, his mind lingered over their lovemaking. The feel of her skin, her mouth, the way she arched her back and took him in fully.

Despite not being with a woman for so long, he was sure Erin was the one woman for him. From the way she fit so perfectly against him, to the way she soothed him, seeming to know exactly what to say and when. It wasn't just that she was a beautiful woman, but also that she was brave, caring, and honest.

Perhaps it was a mistake to make love, he was glad that they'd given in to the pull between them. Something surged through his body at the time. At first he thought it was the arousal, after all, he was making love to a beautiful naked woman. Yet, something different had occurred. It felt as if he'd gained strength from her.

Suddenly, a prickling sensation traveled up and down his extremities, and he shoved his sleeves up to inspect his arms. It was as if ants raced around in circles just under the skin making it warp and smooth in strange patterns.

"What the fuck!" Padriag jumped to his feet and wiped at his arms frantically, but it didn't make a difference. It wasn't painful, quite the opposite. It was as if energy coursed through his veins. He blew out breaths, confused and panicked. Whatever happened was nothing he'd ever seen or experienced.

Since all the men had been rescued, Padriag had admittedly lost much of his appetite. He'd lost weight, which in turn could have affected his magic. Since being with Erin, there had been strangest sensations throughout his body. A pleasant tingling, hunger and lift in spirits.

A shiver set his skin to goosebumps and he lifted his arms to inspect them. Suddenly his body seemed to quiet. Padriag stood, rigid, holding his breath, eyes scanning his arms. Had they'd gotten bigger?

He raced to the back wall where a mirror hung and yanked off his tunic.

"Whoa," his whispered noting that indeed his arms were thicker and chest broader and more muscular. At least an additional inch or two of muscle had piled onto his body.

At least he'd not turned green.

A familiar scent caressed the air, and he inhaled deeply. It was the perfume Erin wore. Padriag let out a breath. Whatever he was to about to face required strength, and somehow the magic that had coursed through Erin had flowed into him.

Now all he had to do was prepare mentally. Somehow, he had to defend himself and manage to stay alive until the others arrived.

He turned and went to the window. The scene outside

was serene, quiet. The aurochs usually made their way into the stables on their own, but Padriag liked to check on them and make sure they had enough food and water.

Perhaps because they were not the object of any predator, aurochs were relatively docile. Padriag hoped they would grow familiar and comfortable around him to make it easier when the time came that he had to saddle and ride one of them.

Sword in hand, he walked out of the house, looking around and taking in every corner or space behind trees as he made his way forward. One could never be too careful.

Chapter Thirteen

A cold shiver made Erin tremble, and she crossed both arms over her chest. When a second wave came, she stood from the sofa and went to a large wicker basket where she kept plush throws. Throwing one over her shoulders, she finished drinking her morning coffee.

This was not the time to get sick, there was so much to get done. It had to be that her flat was chilly. Despite all the upgrades and modernization of the old building, it remained cool. Although extremely well built, the solid structure had not been built to maintain warmth, but to withstand the elements.

There was much to do today. After yoga classes, she and Aubrey were returning to the castle. Dreams had invaded her sleep every night, to the point it felt as if she was living two lives. In her dreams she lived in the alter-world, in a stone fortress. Most of the time, in her dreams, she went about ordinary tasks, but then each night it ended with sounds of men screaming, beasts roaring and the booms of huge boulders hitting the walls.

Unlike what she would do in real life, in the dream she raced to a window and looked out to a surreal scene. Fire-breathing dragons battled against immense horned beasts. Men who were half horses shot arrows at warriors.

Catapults tossed enormous stones into the fray, crushing both man and beast.

Erin screamed in horror, recognizing the warriors in battle. They were the five knights, the men they'd been fighting so hard to save. In her dream, they fought a fruitless battle against formidable opponents.

Just thinking about it sent another shiver through her. What if her dream was a warning, a foretelling of what was to come? If so, it was probably best she talk them out of going back to the alter-realm. Although she always woke up before the battle ended, Erin was positive every single odd was against the men battling in her dream.

THE FIRST YOGA CLASS ENDED, and Erin walked to the front of the studio. The attendees followed discussing plans for the day.

Her mother had not arrived, which was unusual since the one thing everyone could count on no matter what was her mother's punctuality. She'd agreed to cover for Erin for the afternoon, another reason she'd thought her mother would be at the studio by now.

The late morning class was Erin's favorite, and she couldn't keep from smiling as a plume of smoke announced

Evalyn's presence just as the woman paced across the front of the studio. Cigarette in one hand and cell phone in the other, pressed against her ear.

The harried Jane came into view. She waved both hands in the air fanning the smoke away and said something to Evalyn, who showed her the cell phone and returned to her conversation.

Chimes sounded as Jane hurried inside and gave Erin a weary look. "That woman is unbelievable. She's on the phone with her GP, arguing about not wanting to take medication for her high blood pressure, because it's bad for her kidneys while puffing on a cigarette."

Erin nodded. "I don't think any of us will ever understand Evalyn. She is one of a kind."

"Thank goodness for that," Jane said looking around. "Where's Terra?"

"She hasn't arrived yet," Erin replied. "Did you see my mother outside?"

Jane nodded. "Yes, she and Joe are having a very animated discussion about bee keeping."

"Oh no," Erin thought. Her mother was an activist for bee conservation and expansion of wildflower gardens, whilst Joe was deathly allergic to the little creatures.

Just then her mother entered, Joe behind. "Hello darling. I am glad to see that you are at least wearing tinted lip gloss today."

Joe walked past and directly into the studio without a word.

"Mother, you shouldn't argue with Joe," Erin scolded.

"He has a legitimate reason for his fear of bees. How did you even get to that particular topic?"

"He shuddered when he saw the bees on my dress." She motioned to the floral print that was interspersed with cute bees. "I suppose you're right," her mother continued, waving her hand dismissively. "However, whether he has an allergy or not, if the bees are eradicated, he will die with the rest of us."

Evalyn walked in, the smell of cigarette clinging to her. "I am fully booked for the rest of the month," she announced grinning at Erin. "All thanks to you."

"What did Erin do?" her mother asked with a confused expression.

If possible, Evalyn's grin grew wider. "She came for a séance and a spirit possessed me. I hear he made deadly threats. So very exciting."

Her mother's eyes grew round. "Who was it? Who did it threaten?"

"You have to come back. Whatever the entity is may have more to say," Evalyn exclaimed with glee.

"Time to start class." Erin grabbed Evalyn's arm and pulled her into the studio.

"We'll talk after," Evalyn called out to her mother.

On the way to the castle, Erin described her dreams to Aubrey, having to stop mid-sentence, every so often to answer her cousin's questions.

"It seems to me that, since no details change each time, there could be clues that we need to pull from. A hidden message maybe?" Aubrey practically jumped in her seat with excitement. "Or it might be that you will be the hero who saves them all. Especially since you just said you are at the window looking down at all that is happening."

Erin had not considered herself to be any part of the battle, instead of relegated to a role of witness or observer. "There isn't anything I can do to save anyone. The battle seems one-sided against the men. I mean there are dragons and huge beasts fighting against them."

"This is all so interesting, I must admit," Aubrey said. "I still have a hard time believing those hunky men are from medieval times. I mean, they have nice teeth and are pretty clean."

Erin gave her cousin a droll look. "Probably because they became more informed about personal grooming over the years."

"So Padriag ... does he manscape?" Aubrey gave her a mischievous look. "Is he circumcised?"

"Will you stop." Erin couldn't stop the laugher that erupted. "I have no way of knowing."

"Right." Aubrey blew out a breath. "You had that 'just got shagged' look for days after the last time you saw him."

"Look, no mists today," Erin said with too much enthusiasm as the castle came into view.

When she pulled into the narrow road that lead to the front of the castle, Erin stopped the car and let out a long breath. "I have a strange feeling that a lot is about to happen."

Aubrey crossed her arms and shook her head, curls bouncing. "Oh boy."

Chapter Fourteen

Padriag jolted awake and listened intently, unsure if he'd dreamt a loud rumbling sound. Moments later, he sat upright as whatever it was seemed to surge, the sound first distant but then moving closer. It was like a herd of huge animals stampeding over the land.

Apparently, he'd fallen asleep while sitting in front of the fireplace. He considered placing another log on the hearth but changed his mind when, once again, a rumble sounded.

Past the window, there was nothing in sight, the normal snowy ground giving the illusion of peace and quiet as far as he could see. Growing bolder, Padriag opened the front door and peered out. Other than the wind blowing, it was very silent. Most days sounds of small creatures, including bird-like ones, chirped incessantly. At that moment, it was as if every being had gone still, waiting for whatever was headed their way.

Going back inside, Padriag pulled on a hip length, fur-lined coat made of leather, thick boots, straps of daggers.

Finally, he retrieved the sword he'd gotten from over the fireplace and inspected it. He'd spent many hours polishing and sharpening the tool until it not only gleamed brightly, but he could easily split either a hair or a man's skull.

As the rumbling sounds continued, he waited, wondering if perhaps it had nothing to do with him, but was one of those natural things, like earthquakes.

Still, he refused to relax and ignore whatever happened.

It was about half an hour later that the unmistakable sounds of horses approaching made him peer out the window.

On horseback, warriors wearing black armor and swords strapped to their back lined up in a half circle surrounding the front of the home. There were probably as many men around the back half.

Padriag's blood ran ice-cold. There was only one reason Meliot would send this many. The wizard wanted him captured and brought to him alive. Despite Meliot's surprisingly reckless decisions at times, the wizard wasn't stupid. The man had his reasons for whatever would happen next. If Padriag had to guess, it could be that the evil man knew something about the others returning, and he hoped to capture them as well. Or the wizard wished to ensure that he and Liam became trapped in the current realm forever.

Annoyed that he'd been complacent in not constantly strengthening the warding around the house, Padriag lowered the wooden plank to latch the door. Not that wood would keep the enemy out, but it would slow them down. Padriag lifted his hands, power forming in his palms as he began the warding spell.

Magic sparked and a luminescent and clear barrier began forming with wavy walls reminiscent of a water bubble.

Before the ward could fully close, the front door flew open with a burst of light, and moments later warriors poured into the room, swords in hand.

Padriag was just a couple steps from his blade, the only way to reach it without chancing a stab to his back was to use magic. Cupping his hands, he moved them outward forming a fiery shield.

Seeing what he did, the dark warriors surged toward him, and he shot bursts of power at them using both hands. Energy pulses raced from his palms sending several of them tumbling backward.

He scrambled away from them and reached for his sword, considering whether, perhaps, the magic worked better than his blade.

The dark warriors parted, and a tall, muscular one walked into the room. "Meliot sent us to fetch you. He has questions." The warrior wore a helmet, so Padriag couldn't see the features. It could be he was human, or someone from that realm. Hard to tell.

"Yeah. No. Tell him I've got other plans. Maybe next time." Padriag sheathed his sword as energy sizzled from his palms.

Through the eyeholes of the helmet, the warrior's gaze focused on Padriag's hands. "Do you think your weak magic will win against us? We are fortified with much stronger magic."

Padriag shrugged. "Have you ever considered that all you

exist for is to do some old guy's bidding? When was the last time you took a self-care day?"

The warrior took a step forward and Padriag blasted him with both hands, sending a combination of energy and fire. Despite taking a couple steps backward, Meliot's warrior didn't fall. The fact that the man could withstand what had sent all the others tumbling backwards was troubling.

Once again, Padriag sent energy to his palms.

"If you come willingly, we will not beat you the entire way there," the warrior said in a bored tone. "It spoils the fun, but I will make that concession."

"Aren't you a sweetie," Padriag said and once again sent energy and flames at the warrior. This time the guy didn't even flinch.

"Damn it," Padriag pulled his sword and held it with both hands. "I am not going willingly."

"So be it," the warrior unsheathed his own sword and advanced. The odds were fully against Padriag, but he would fight to the death.

The warrior went for an overhead strike and Padriag blocked it and jabbed forward with his own, barely missing the man's midsection. When the warrior struck again, metal clashed against metal, sending vibrations down Padriag's arms.

Gritting his teeth, he managed to shove the warrior away. Swords swinging, they moved in a circle, neither getting the best of the other. Thankfully, the other warriors did not intercede, although Padriag had no doubt they would if by some miracle, the larger dark warrior fell.

A hard strike to the back of his head made Padriag see

stars. He barely was able to block a strike from his opponent. They would not fight fair, it was a losing battle. Padriag understood, but damn if he was going to just relinquish control.

In one fluid motion, he sliced the air in the direction of his opponent whilst pulling a dagger from the strap across his chest. He whirled and flung the weapon, satisfied when it sunk into the chest of one of the idiots behind him.

He turned back just in time to block another blow.

Once again Padriag was hit from behind, this time so hard his knees buckled. Before he could catch himself, another strike to the back of his head barely registered as everything went black.

"Find out where the rip in the realm's wall is. I must know how he was able to leave and re-enter from the other side," a deep, familiar voice penetrated the fog in Padriag's head.

He had sunk to his knees, his arms outstretched, shackles that hung from a beam overhead around his wrists. The discomfort of his shoulders practically coming out of their sockets was nothing compared to the burning pain on his entire back and the pulsing of his fingertips now devoid of nails.

He'd lost count of the different methods of torture he'd been subjected to. Many times he'd slipped on his own pool of blood as the sting of a whip across his back had continued until he'd lost consciousness. Was it two or three times now that he'd passed out? He couldn't be sure.

Pretending to remain unconscious, he opened his eyes just enough to see who Meliot spoke to. It was the same warrior he'd fought back at the cabin.

"If he has not spoken by now, he will not be forthcoming no matter what we do to him," the warrior replied. Padriag couldn't place the accent, German perhaps.

Meliot growled. "I do not want the opinion of a traitorous slug like you." The wizard whirled to face Padriag, and he met his gaze.

"Don't let me interrupt your family squabble. But the slug is right, I will not tell you anything. Mainly because I have no fucking idea what the hell you're talking about." Voice barely audible, Padriag began coughing, his throat raw from screaming.

Meliot closed the distance between them, the bottomless black eyes digging into his. No matter how many times he'd had the misfortune of being confronted by the wizard, the malevolence emanating from him made Padriag's skin crawl. He could live another three hundred years and never forget what being in the presence of pure evil felt like.

"You are keeping secrets. Perhaps about the others, or it could be you are hiding something. What is it?" Meliot leaned forward grabbed Padriag's hair and yanked him forward. Padriag couldn't keep from moaning at the stretching of his shoulders and open wounds on his back.

"Tell me what you know, and I will let you go free." Meliot's voice echoed in his ears, swirling around his head like smoke.

Padriag tried to pull back, but it was in vain. Not only did Meliot have a good grip on his hair, but he was weak from being tortured. "Even if I knew anything, I wouldn't tell you," he rasped.

The wizard's eyes narrowed. "Soon you will be too weak to guard your thoughts. Then you will gladly share everything to stop the pain. The beautiful pain that you should be embracing."

Before Meliot could delve into his mind, Padriag warded himself. His magic couldn't compete against Meliot's, especially now that the evil wizard's powers had strengthened. But thankfully he could still ward his mind.

Letting out a long hiss of annoyance, the wizard slapped him hard across the face with so much force Padriag was surprised his head remained attached. "You are a fool! You will die here in my dungeons."

Meliot whirled around and motioned to the guard who'd stood by the door. The man looked familiar. With blond hair and bright blue eyes, he stood tall, at least six foot four.

"Put him in the cage. No food or water." The wizard looked at Padriag. "I suggest salt water to clean his wounds." With that he swept from the room leaving the two men alone.

"You should tell him what you know. He will not stop until you do," the guard said in a flat voice.

Padriag managed to stand, his shoulders still pained him, but not as much. "Is that what you did. Gave in? Betrayed others?" He couldn't keep the accusatory tone from his statement.

Ignoring him, the guard walked to a long table where various implements of torture were kept and grabbed a sack of what Padriag assumed was salt.

Padriag entire body quaked, anticipating the pain he was about to endure. When the warrior walked toward him, he closed his eyes and braced himself.

"This should help with the healing," the guard said and slowly poured liquid down Padriag's back and smoothed something across it with fast precise moves. It smarted and he gritted his teeth, but it wasn't anywhere as intolerable as he'd expected. He let out a long breath in relief.

First one shackle and then the next was unlocked and his arms hung limply at his sides.

"Can you walk?" The guard pushed him forward.

Padriag stumbled, barely able to stay upright. "I will walk," he said and took a wobbly step forward, then another. His parched, aching throat made it painful to swallow. He longed for a swallow of water. It would be useless to ask.

The guard took his arm and pulled him forward, out of the room and down steeps stairs. Several times, Padriag lost his footing and would have fallen if not for the guard's strong hold.

Once reaching the bottom of the second set of stairs, they emerged into the darkness outside the castle.

By this time, Padriag would have been hard pressed to keep moving, and the guard was practically carrying him.

"Where are you taking me?" he panted the words, terrified that the cage was outside, and he'd be left naked and injured in the freezing cold.

The guard pushed him forward and he collapsed on all fours, the surroundings became blurry, he was losing consciousness. A mixture of emotions surged, and he prayed not to wake up. Death was a hundred times better than going through the torture again.

"I cannot do more for you." The guard's voice permeated through the edges of his mind. "Go to the cottage, you will be safe there."

Padriag used the very last of his reserve to dematerialize.

He landed in a heap in the log cabin, crawled to lay in front of the fire as darkness enveloped him.

Chapter Fifteen

Aubrey chose not to remain in the library at the castle as everyone discussed and tried to make sense of Erin's dreams. They'd decided to stay the night. In truth, she considered leaving and returning to her own home. After all, there was nothing she could contribute, other than being there for Erin.

It was a beautiful day, so moments later, with a cup of tea in hand, Aubrey went outside to a set of tables and chairs and sat down. There had been so much on her mind lately, this situation with Erin being one of them.

As much as she loved her huge home, with it came a myriad of tasks. Maintenance and repairs were full-time jobs in themselves. Thankfully, her father made provisions that paid for a gardener and a maid service. However, the list of repairs, veterinary appointments for the horses and other estate management issues was becoming overwhelming.

She loved Ashcraig Hall, but at the same time Aubrey wanted to make her own mark, to grow the yoga business she and Erin owned. Lately she'd considered purchasing a smaller home and asking her father if perhaps they should sell the estate.

She had one brother, Stuart, a musician who lived in Glasgow. Stuart's band was gaining popularity and was in high demand in the city. Her brother had no interest in moving to the country, and had made it clear he had no desire to live in the house.

The gust of wind whirled around her, and she lifted her face to the sun, closing her eyes. Her heart ached at the thought of moving from the family estate, yet perhaps going flat hunting with Erin had made her wish to live closer to the city, within walking distance of shops and restaurants.

The moment she opened her eyes, a startled scream ripped from Aubrey's throat. The ceramic cup slipped from her fingers, shattering against the cold paving stones at the feet of a massive blond man.

He was a mountain of muscle, his presence so imposing that it sent a jolt of fear through her veins. His piercing blue eyes locked onto hers, brows shooting up in surprise, as if he was just as shocked to see her as she was to see him.

"Who are you?" His voice was rough, laced with a heavy accent that made the hairs on her arms rise.

"Who the hell are you?" Aubrey shot to her feet so fast that blood rushed to her head, making her sway.

The stranger reached out, his calloused fingers catching her arm to steady her. She recoiled instantly, jerking away as if his touch had burned her. "I can stand on my own," she snapped.

His gaze flickered toward the house, his expression

unreadable. From the way he dressed—dark leather, a belt weighed down with weapons, a tunic stitched with unfamiliar symbols—Aubrey knew immediately. He had to be from the other realm.

She took a cautious step back, her heart hammering. "You're not from this world, are you?"

"No."

Aubrey's mind spun as she calculated the distance to the door. If she ran, would she make it before he caught her?

Before she could act, the blond warrior lifted a hand, as if sensing her intent. "I am not here to take you," he said, his voice steady, as if soothing a skittish animal. He motioned to the doorway. "I bring a message."

"Give it to them yourself," Aubrey shot back before she could stop herself. Defiance was her knee-jerk reaction, the very reason she struggled to take orders from anyone and had to work for herself. "They're inside."

A muscle ticked in his jaw, and he exhaled as though summoning patience. It was then she noticed a jagged scar down the left side of his face.

At her perusal, he gave her a droll, almost amused look. "I am called Gunther. I serve Meliot."

At the mention of that name, Aubrey's blood turned to ice. Meliot. The wizard. The man whose very name carried whispers of death.

Her breath hitched. He was here to kill her.

Spinning on her heel, she lunged for the door, but steel-like arms wrapped around her, yanking her back against his solid chest. A rough hand clamped over her mouth.

"Will you listen to me?" His voice rumbled with irritation.

Aubrey let out a muffled snarl and drove her heel into his shin. He grunted in pain, his grip not loosening, if anything it felt tighter.

"Tell them," he ground out, "their friend is gravely wounded. Meliot will find him again soon. I did what I could to guard my house, but it will not hold for long."

Aubrey stilled. A warning. Was he telling the truth? Or was this a carefully laid trap?

She went limp in his grasp. He loosened his hold just slightly—enough for her to twist free. She whirled, making another break for the house, but his strong hand closed around her wrist, spinning her back to face him. His blue eyes locked onto hers, filled with something strange. Not cruelty. Not malice. Something else. When his bright blue gaze traveled over her, Aubrey stopped breathing. There was something like desire in his eyes and damn if it didn't affect her in all the wrong places.

"Who are you?" he asked, this time not with suspicion, but genuine curiosity.

"The woman who's going to kick you again if you don't stop grabbing me," she shot back, jerking her arm free.

Something flickered in his gaze before he dipped his head. "I helped the knight escape. But I can do no more, not without risking my own life."

Aubrey narrowed her eyes. "Right. So you serve the wizard, but now you suddenly have a conscience? What, you woke up this morning and decided to be a hero?"

His throat bobbed, and he lowered his head slightly, as if ashamed. "Something like that."

For the first time, hesitation softened the hard angles of his face. When he looked up again, regret shadowed his features. "I could do a thousand good deeds, and it would never be enough. I will never be redeemed. Nor do I deserve to be."

Aubrey parted her lips to fire back another sharp remark, but no words came.

If he had truly done what he claimed ... if he had saved Padraig ...

She swallowed hard. "If you're telling the truth—thank you."

Gunther gave a small nod, then, without another word, vanished into thin air.

Aubrey gasped, staggering back. Her pulse thundered in her ears.

"That did not just happen." She stared at the shattered cup at her feet, her hands trembling. "Oh my god. It did."

She turned and sprinted for the house, shoving the door open with a bang. Barreling through the halls, she burst into the library, where a cluster of familiar faces turned toward her in alarm.

"Padraig is in terrible danger!"

Every eye locked on her. Not only were Gwen and her sisters present, but also John and the four men who had been trapped with Padraig.

"What happened?" Liam demanded, already on his feet.

Aubrey hesitated for just a fraction of a second. Would they believe her? She almost snorted at the absurdity of her doubt. These were people who had crossed from one world to another—yet she was still questioning her own sanity?

"A man," she blurted. "Gunther. He showed up outside. He said Padraig was in danger."

Tammie gasped audibly and looked to a wide-eyed Erin. "Gunther? That was his name, wasn't it? The man who took me and Erin. He kidnapped us and brought us to Meliot's castle."

Erin nodded, her gaze darting to Aubrey. "Did he hurt you?"

"No I'm fine."

John's gaze darkened. "And now he shows up with a message? That doesn't make sense."

"It could be a trap," Liam muttered, his expression grim.

"Tell us everything," Tristan said, his voice calm but urgent. "Exactly what happened."

Aubrey exhaled shakily, recounting every detail—Gunther's warning, his expression of torment, his cryptic words. By the time she finished, her legs felt weak, and she sank into a chair, exhaustion pressing down on her.

But one thought still gnawed at her.

Had Gunther really betrayed his master?

Or was this just another piece of Meliot's game?

KNOWING that Aubrey had been in danger made Erin's stomach hurt. The last thing she wanted was for her cousin to be hurt because of the strange situation she'd fallen into. Unfortunately, as much as she wanted to ask her cousin to stay away from the situation until it was all sorted, Aubrey had now become part of it.

After repeating every word Gunther had spoken and ensuring that she didn't leave out even the smallest of details, Aubrey sat back, exhausted. "He disappeared, and then I ran in here."

"Wait," Gwen said, holding up a hand and getting everyone's attention. "Erin, in the dreams you see yourself inside a building. There is a battle outside. When you look out, you see these men, fighting."

"Yes," Erin nodded, picturing the events of her dream. "They fight against creatures that look like centaurs. There are dragons in the air and huge beasts battling too."

Gwen looked into her eyes. "Erin, think. Are the dragons fighting the centaurs and other beasts, or the men?"

"I-I am not sure." She wanted to cry. Despite the dream having repeated, she'd not considered that some of the mystical beasts could be allies. "They fly in circles, their fiery blasts aimed downward. Closing her eyes, she brought the images of what she saw outside the window to mind. Instantly the fantastical scene came to life. The strange color of the sky and trees that looked like they came out of a Dr. Suess book were more than real. The men fought below her window, swords slicing, shields held up.

Liam and Padriag shot arrows, striking the advancing centaurs, some falling, some continuing forward despite arrows protruding from their bodies. There are hundreds of men in black armor fighting with the centaurs, and the five men were more than outnumbered. She concentrated for a long time, committing as much as she could to memory.

Her eyes flew open. "The dragons are attacking the dark side."

"I must go," Liam said then looked at the other men. "As soon as you feel the compulsion, make sure you are armed before returning.

The handsome Englishman went to John and took his hand, together they walked out from the room to say a private goodbye.

"Maybe, I should go with him," Erin said. "I could help care for Padriag."

"No!" Aubrey exclaimed, fear making her throat constrict. "You cannot possibly be serious. What if you get stuck there?"

Erin felt as if on the brink of tears. "I want to help," she said softly.

Gwen covered her hand. "If anything you will be a hindrance at battle, with the men having to worry about keeping you safe while fighting. Stay here with us, at the castle. We will wait together."

"I'll have to go to my flat and get clothes." Erin looked to Aubrey. "Can you cover for me at the studio?"

"Of course. I'll tell your Mum that you're doing a yoga retreat at a castle. Last minute thing." Aubrey smiled widely at having come up with a lie so easily.

They left the castle shortly after Liam dematerialized, both letting out a long breath once ensconced in Erin's car.

"Are you sure you're alright?" Erin asked her cousin.

Aubrey nodded. "Everything about this," she motioned to the castle. "Is surreal, but strangely, I have something like a déjà vu feeling about this, as if I have seen it all before."

"I hope you are not meant to be another part of this. At least the guy, Gunther, didn't take you, like he did me. I can't help thinking about what you said. That he seemed honest."

They sat in the car in silence for a long moment, Erin unsure of whether she should remain at the castle or stay away. After all, either way, there was little she could do to help. On impulse she opened the door.

"Did you forget something?" Aubrey asked.

Erin shook her head. "I feel that you and I should stay together. I think it's best if we return to your house, I can commute easily both to the studio and to the castle and be at either one in less than an hour."

The relief on Aubrey's face confirmed her suspicions. Her cousin was afraid, both for Erin and for herself. Seeing one of Meliot's henchmen face-to-face was not something one got over easily.

Chapter Sixteen

Despite the warmth of the crackling fire and the thick rug beneath him, pain pulsed through Padraig's battered body, each wound felt as if his skin was on fire. His eyes fluttered open to the dim light of flames in the hearth flickering across the cabin's interior.

A violent shudder shook through Padraig, his body trapped in the cruel cycle of fever one moment burning from the inside out, to the next seized by a bone-deep chill that made his teeth chatter.

He swallowed against the raw dryness in his throat. He would give anything—*anything*—for a cup of water. The thirst clawed at him, nearly as unbearable as the pain cutting through his back and hands. Frustration burned behind his eyes, and a few stray tears splashed onto the rug beneath him. He did not weep out of self-pity but out of sheer helplessness.

If only he had strengthened the wards on the house. If

only he had stayed in Esland. His life would have been boring, perhaps even lonely, but at least it would not have been an unrelenting game of survival, a constant struggle against Meliot's sadistic whims.

If he was to remain in this cursed alter-world, he would have to find a way to disappear, to vanish so completely that even Meliot's unnatural reach could not drag him back to his torture chamber.

Padriag did not believe for one moment that the guard had freed him out of kindness. No, this was Meliot's design, to release him, set him free just long enough to recover, and then send his soulless guards to retrieve him.

A sharp pain sliced through him as he shifted, pressing both palms to the floor and forcing himself upright. His back screamed in protest, torn flesh stretching painfully, but he clenched his jaw and endured it. The simple act of sitting drained what little strength he had, leaving him breathless and trembling.

His gaze drifted toward the adjoining room, where a pewter pitcher of water sat atop the rustic table. He imagined gripping it, tilting it to his lips, and drinking every drop. Another form of torture because in his current state, it was impossible to get that far.

Then, out of the corner of his eye, he noticed something —just within reach. A mug, tall and sturdy, sat beside the hearth.

Dragging himself forward, ignoring the sharp protest of his wounds, Padriag stretched out a shaking hand and grasped the handle. The heat of it stung his palm, but he hardly cared. Lifting it to his lips, he caught the sharp scent of herbs—*willow bark and bog myrtle*. He knew their properties well. Pain relief. Fever reduction.

Poison? It could be, but he doubted Meliot would allow him a merciful death.

The tea was bitter and strong, steeped far too long, but he welcomed its warmth as it slid down his throat, easing the unbearable dryness. He let his head fall back against the nearest chair, eyes drifting toward the wooden beams above. He needed to get off the floor, needed his strength back.

A flicker of memory surfaced.

The guard.

What had he said? Something about Padraig being safe there?

He turned his head slightly, eyes landing on the coat of arms mounted above the fireplace. Dutch. That made sense —the guard's accent, his features.

Janssen.

When Padriag had been in Esland, Sterling had mentioned Janssen and called him a friend. If that were true, then once, perhaps long ago, Janssen had been an honorable man. Had he, too, been cast into this cursed realm by Meliot? And if so, what had broken him? What could turn a man into the loyal servant of a monster?

Padraig let his eyes slide shut, the fever dragging at him. He had to find out more about Janssen. He had to talk to Sterling.

If there was still a shred of the man Janssen had once been, perhaps he would help Padriag thwart Meliot's plans.

. . .

A DAY OR TWO PASSED. Padriag managed to pull a thick blanket over himself. From the stinging of the wounds on his back, he'd torn some open. They were probably bleeding. The tea had given him some relief from the pain, and the fever had finally broken.

How many hours or days it had been since he'd been returned to the cabin, he couldn't be sure of. He worried about the aurochs, that they'd been penned in the stables for who knew how long and whether they had food and water.

Judging by the dimmed light outside, the suns were setting, marking the end of the current day. Padriag promised himself he'd be well enough to go out and see about the animals in the morning and allowed himself the respite of sleep.

"Padriag. Padriag." Something or someone was shaking him awake. Clenching his jaw at the pain that would come, Padriag closed his right hand into a fist and swung.

"Ouch. That was bloody unnecessary," Liam yelled.

"Shit. Sorry." Padriag looked up at the Brit massaging his jaw. "I am so glad to see you."

Liam gave him a droll look. "You could have fooled me." A frown formed as his friend looked at him. "You look like … horrible."

"And you haven't seen the best parts yet," Padriag replied. "I need water. I would get it except my legs don't work that well and I may be stuck to the rug."

Instead of retrieving the water, Liam leaned forward to examine him closer. "I should have stayed here. To help. What happened?"

Glancing toward the pitcher, Padriag closed his eyes. "Water please."

He waited for Liam to pour water and bring him a cup. He drained it and held it out for a refill. "Is there any food left?"

"I'll cook something," Liam said. "First let me look at your wounds and clean them."

For what seemed like an eternity, Liam meticulously cleaned his wounds adding a poultice to help keep infection away, then wrapped Padriag's upper half with strips of fabric cut from a thin blanket.

It was only after helping him into a tunic that fell to his knees that Liam helped Padriag to one of the overstuffed chairs and then pulled a small table close.

The aroma of whatever bubbled on the wood stove made Padriag's mouth water. The bowl of steaming stew Liam placed on the table brought actual tears to his eyes.

"Can you see about the aurochs? I am not sure if they have any feed or water," Padriag asked.

Despite obviously wishing to know what had occurred that left Padriag so injured, Liam stood and left the house. Alone again, Padriag sagged. Grateful did not begin to describe what he'd been through at the moment. If not for Liam, he wasn't sure how long he would have had to wait before being able to walk to fetch water and food for himself. He would have forced himself, but it would have been slow going.

When Liam returned, he lowered across from him. "They had feed left, but I had to refill their water. I'll let them out in the morning." The Brit shook his head. "They are menacing creatures. The way their eyes shine will take time to get used to."

"You can't stay," Padriag stated. "It's too dangerous. I am certain Meliot will send his minions again. I am sure the only reason I was released was so that I can suffer more, having to take care of myself."

"He didn't ask about me?" Liam gave him a quizzical look. "As far as we know, he is not aware my curse was broken."

"He did. I told him you'd gone to Esland. Since it wasn't exactly a lie, he believed it."

"What else did he ask about?"

Padriag met Liam's pale blue eyes. "He insists there is a tear in the wall between the realms. He demanded I tell him where it is. I overheard him telling one of the guards that he had to be the first to find it."

Liam's eyebrows flew upward. "If that is true, he wants to be able to go to the other side. To wreak havoc there, to spread his darkness."

"That would be bad." Padriag was aware 'bad' was a vast understatement. If Meliot was able to move between the realms, he could possibly gain more power through the energy of the gateway. If it happened, the warlock would be unstoppable.

"I am here to stay," Liam said motioning to a large sack on the end of the table. "It's been foretold that all of us must return if we are to stop him."

Ire rose and Padriag pushed his bowl away. "It could be

that you and the others return only to die. Don't do it. Please go back and keep the others from coming."

"I believe the tides are turning. Everything is in motion for what comes and what happens next is part of a larger plan. We cannot stop what must be. The others will come even against their will. No one can stop the progression of what is foretold."

Rolling his eyes, Padriag looked at Liam. "You ruined the entire delivery of your little speech. Should have put on a hooded cloak and added a cackle at the end."

"There is something you should know," Liam said ignoring his comment. "A man called Gunther came to Scotland, the castle, with a message."

"That Viking looking man is who helped me escape. This must be his cottage. I don't trust him," Padriag replied. "What did he say?"

"He appeared outside, scaring Aubrey, Erin's cousin, half to death. He informed her that you were injured and required help."

"I still don't trust him," Padriag insisted. "I believe the only reason they let me go was so that I can suffer through healing and then they'd come for me again."

"Aubrey said he seemed genuinely concerned for you." The Brit got up and served himself stew. "Whether he is trustworthy or not, the man did come and ask that we help you."

Padriag yawned. "I am going to try to get some sleep."

"Drink this first," Liam lifted a kettle from the stove and poured more of the same tea into a cup. "I assume the tea was left here by Gunther."

"Probably," Padriag quipped then drank every drop of tea.

MEN TALKING WOKE Padriag the next day. By the brightness of the suns, he could tell it was late morning. Someone was there. Every movement was excruciating, like claws scraping down his back. When he finally managed to sit on the edge of the bed, bare feet on the floor, he had to take several breaths, willing the throbbing to stop.

Not that he stood a chance against an able-bodied opponent, still Padriag held a dagger in each hand as he slowly made his way to the voices. It was only after hearing a soft chuckle that he relaxed, recognizing it was Tristan.

It was happening. What Liam had foreseen, that the others would return, would face an enemy so strong, it could cost their lives. He wasn't sure if it was guilt or pride that filled him. If they were to die, then they would die together. None of them, for one instant, backing down.

The sorceress who'd granted them powers to defend themselves had predicted that on the last day of the three hundredth year in the alter-world, they would become mortal. It was a price they'd gladly accepted, convinced they'd find their way back long before the deadline.

"You should be in bed," Liam said when Padriag limped into the front room. "Your wounds will heal if you stay still."

Padriag ignored him and looked at Tristan. The laird was a different man since leaving, his hair was cut into a modern style. Unlike the man who'd been trapped for three hundred years, his tunic, leather breeches and animal hide boots were replaced with sturdy denim pants, a thick pullover and a jacket that could withstand artic temperature. On his feet, Tristan wore rugged mountain boots. He was more than prepared.

"After we leave, you can plan a trip to the north pole," Padriag quipped by way of greeting.

Tristan gave him a puzzled look. Sometimes Padriag forgot that they were from another time and had so much to learn about the world. Unlike him who'd often gone to Scotland, had sat in university classes, kept up with the changing times, the others had for the most part remained separate from their homeland.

"Liam told me what happened. We should have been here to defend you." Tristan's tone was flat, his gaze roaming over Padriag.

Padriag shrugged. "Been there done that. Although I must admit, Meliot was very creative this time." He held up a hand with its half-healed wounds. "No fingernails."

Ever methodical, Liam motioned to the table. "Come sit. I made more of that tea for you. Tell us everything you remember about the surroundings at Meliot's."

LIAM TOOK Tristan outside to see the aurochs as Padriag sat in front of the hearth feeling restless. He wanted to prepare for the battle ahead, but it proved difficult since he was barely able to move without pain. Besides moving too much would reopen the lash wounds.

"This is not what I expected," Gavin stated, materializing. When he took a step forward, his boot caught the edge of the rug, and he stumbled forward.

"If you land on me, I will kill you," Padriag held both arms out hoping to stop the huge blond man's fall.

Somehow Gavin managed to not fall and gave Padriag a triumphant grin. "How are you?"

"Excited that I don't have to worry about trimming my fingernails for a while." Padraig held up his hands.

"He tries to be creative." Gavin said with a grimace.

Blowing out a breath, Padriag shrugged. "He wanted to keep things fresh between us."

"I have a new power," Gavin said. "Last night, when I was working at the stables, the sorceress appeared to me. She told me to hold my arms out." He removed a jacket like Tristan's and rolled up his sleeves. Then he held out his arms that had what looked like tribal tattoos had formed from the wrist upward. "I can send energy bursts from my palms. Much like yours."

"Holy shit," Padriag exclaimed. "That's amazing."

The Scot studied his arms. "Need to practice." He looked around the room. "Where are the others?"

"At the stables, looking at the Esland aurochs."

After stating he'd return, Gavin hurried from the house. Nothing like a new creature to get men's attention.

"You look like shite." Niall's deep voice cut through the still air, startling Padriag from his daze. His tone was laced with wry amusement, though concern flickered beneath it. "Let's hope my power of healing returns with me."

Before Padriag could form a reply, Niall stepped forward, his presence steady and resolute. Warmth radiated from his palms as he pressed them against Padriag's battered skin, and the reaction was immediate—like fire and ice colliding in his veins. A sharp, tingling sensation raced through him, then a rush of relief, as if invisible threads were knitting his torn flesh back together.

Without even glancing down, he knew—the wounds were closing.

His fingertips mending.

Healing completely.

Chapter Seventeen

Despite having led the morning yoga class, Erin was restless, her mind on what was occurring in the alter-world. Yes, it was a dangerous, even deadly place to be, still she wished to be there. Anything was better than not knowing.

There was no telling how long it would be before the men returned. Or when she and the others would know for certain their fate had been sealed, and they'd remain in the alter-world. The last malevolent and cruel punishment by Meliot.

She'd been at the castle the night before, finding that all the men were gone. Everyone had dematerialized in the order they'd been rescued, Niall being the last. Although Tammie greeted her pleasantly, when she entered the library, the undercurrent of desperate hope was tangible.

"We will cast spells of power and triumph," Gwen, her tone resolute as she had motioned Erin to join them around a table. The place where they always labored over the long and arduous task of saving five men who'd bravely persevered in a world not their own. The men deserved more than freedom for all they'd gone through. If fate was kind, Tristan, Gavin, Liam, Niall and Padriag should be granted peaceful, happy and healthy long lives.

"Hello, dear." A cheerful greeting brought her out of her musings, her memories of the castle fading as her mother entered the studio.

Erin smiled brightly, studying her mother's colorful ensemble of purples, greens and hues of orange. The long flowing skirts, topped with a loose lime-green blouse, somehow came together beautifully.

"You have such an eye for color." Erin hugged her mother. "You're early today."

Her mother nodded. "Perhaps menopause or something else, but I have been waking early.

"You look rested. Are you all right?"

With a slight shrug, her mother shook her head. "I feel fine. I'll take a nap later. How was your retreat?"

For a moment, Erin was at a loss for words. "Oh look there's Evalyn smoking again," She said with a bit too much enthusiasm.

"Ugh." Her mother stalked to the door and went outside. Then without a moment's hesitation, her mother plucked the offensive item from Evalyn's hand, tossed it to the ground and smashed it with her shoe.

Erin clasped a hand over her mouth and laughed when Evalyn stared at her mother with wide eyes and mouth open. For the first time since she'd known the cranky woman, she seemed to have met her match.

The women then walked inside, Evalyn looking crestfallen as they went into the studio.

Left alone, Erin's thoughts immediately went to Padriag. If only there was a way to know what happened.

Erin looked up at the ceiling forcing herself to push all thoughts aside. There would be time to ponder and discuss upon returning to the castle.

Driving toward the castle that afternoon, Erin lost track of time, her mind already on what had to be done once she arrived there. Somehow, she knew they were getting close to a breakthrough. Everyone had felt it the night before, an almost tangible electricity in the air. It had been as if they'd somehow reached the alter-world.

The road seemed to go on forever, nothing in sight. Erin looked around confused. She'd passed Culross a while ago, the castle usually came into view shortly after. Had she somehow driven past it, while musing about the day before?

She pulled over and maneuvered her car around. Surely she'd gone past the castle. The road looked unfamiliar with vegetation on both sides of the road and no buildings in sight.

Once she headed back and drove for what seemed like half an hour, she pulled over again. Nothing looked familiar. It could be that she had accidentally turned off the main route somewhere but there were no roads cutting to either side.

"What did you do Erin?" she chided herself with a

grimace. It was almost four o'clock in the afternoon, a bit later than she usually arrived, but not so late that the others would worry. The navigation system showed a straight road, no turns, no other roads. Slowly, she opened the car door and slid out.

Although the sun shone, it was a chilly day, the brisk wind blowing across the road making colder. Erin turned in a full circle. "Where the hell am I?"

As if in reply, the horizon shimmied, blurring before becoming clear again. Stumbling backward, Erin covered her mouth as dread coursed down her spine. It was a magic trick. Meliot once again blocking her from going to the castle.

It meant they were getting close to breaking the spell, but it also meant that she must be the one holding the key, the one who could bring the warlock down.

When a strange sound like the crackle of thunder sounded, she hurried back into the car and let out a shaky breath.

"What is it?" She asked out loud. "What do I have that he fears?" Her hands trembling, she gripped the steering wheel.

If going straight in two directions wasn't working, then she'd take a chance and go in another. Pushing on the gas, she went forward and then yanked the steering wheel to the right, letting out a scream as the car bumped over the uneven terrain on the side of the road.

The view of bushes and fence evaporated, and she let out another scream veering the car to the left to avoid hitting a cow and guided the car back to the road. She was less than a mile from the castle, the edifice looming in the short distance. Seeing it, she let out a sniffle and blinked back tears.

Thoughts and ideas whirling in her head, Erin came to a stop just in front of the main door, threw it into park and rushed into the building. It was only when the door closed behind her that she let out a shaky breath.

"There you are," Sabrina called out, walking past with a cup of tea in each hand. "I can't wait to tell you what we've experienced."

Erin followed, unsure she wanted to hear anything more. How had she come to be in the midst of such a strange situation?

Upon entering the library, she continued past the others to the sideboard. Uncorking a decanter, she poured whiskey into a short glass and drank it down in one gulp. She sputtered as the strong liquid burned past her throat. Then she poured a second. "Whatever you are going to tell me. Bet you I can one-up it."

Four sets of eyes followed her as she joined them at the table.

"That fucking wizard tried to block me from coming here. I drove for an hour up and down a long road with no turnoff and no views of anything but bushes and sky. I almost hit a cow, when I drove blindly into the horizon." Erin sat back in the chair and crossed her arms over her chest. "What you got?"

"Whoa," Tammie said. "What happened here is pretty interesting, but no cows involved."

John's somber gaze met hers. "You have the key to breaking the spell. Whatever it is, it's already in your possession."

"Of course," Erin said. "I don't suppose you know what it is."

They all shook their heads. Gwen pulled her long black locks up and expertly wrapped the strands into a practiced top knot, holding it in place with a floral scrunchy. "We do not, hopefully we will find out today. We've written down some things we can try but were waiting for you to arrive before we attempt them. Do you have any ideas?"

"None."

"Very well, let's try a finding spell." Gwen gave her a warm smile. "Close your eyes and try to relax. When you see a small light, focus on it."

Erin closed her eyes and waited, sure enough a tiny yellowish light appeared. Concentrating on it, she opened her mind to whatever would come.

When the others began speaking out words, she couldn't quite make out what they said. In the darkness something round came into view. It was like a ball, but yellow, it floated without moving. The air smelled of water, not sea water, but more like that of a loch. The yellow ball flattened and began transforming, its shape elongating and changing from yellow to gold. A dagger formed, the hilt a dark gold, the blade darkening to an even deeper shade.

Then it burst into pieces, the shards flying in all directions like a firework. The vision broke apart, and she opened her eyes.

"Is there a dagger here, one with a golden handle?"

"If there is, we'll find it." Tammie looked around the table. "Where would Tristan keep swords, daggers and such?"

Gwen frowned. "He took his sword and pair of daggers with him. None of them were gold."

"If you already have it, then it could be at your home," John said. "If it's Padriag's ancestral home, then he could have placed it somewhere on the property."

"That's true," Erin replied. "But where to look? My flat was totally empty when I moved in. There is much more to the house. It's divided into two flats. We can't search my landlord's home without her permission and that would entail having a believable explanation."

"We will try yours, and last ditch we can find a way to convince your landlord to agree to a search of hers," Sabrina announced and held out the spell book that had been instrumental in helping to break the men's curses. "With this, I am sure we will find the dagger."

Everyone got up and began donning coats, shoving papers and materials they'd need for spellcasting into backpacks and satchels. Within a few moments, they were ready to go.

Erin pulled on her coat. "When this is over, I'm going on holiday and basking in the sun for a month."

UPON ARRIVING AT HER FLAT, they entered, and each person found a place to sit on her couch and chairs in the front room. Erin didn't have a large table. The one in the kitchen was shoved against the wall, leaving only enough seating for three.

"I will put the kettle on," she announced, going into

hostess mode. She opened a cabinet and pulled out a sleeve of biscuits and placed the sweet treats on a plate.

"You don't have to do this," Tammie said, taking the plate form her hands with a knowing smile. "Come into the other room. Each of us can make our own tea, if we want some."

Gwen looked to Erin. "Is there anything you own that is in the shape of a dagger? Perhaps a jewelry piece?"

Erin shook her head. "I don't wear much jewelry. Only a pair of diamond earrings my parents gave me for my twenty-first birthday and a locket that once belonged to my grandmother. It's inscribed with a rose and leaves."

Sabrina opened the books of spells. "There is a spell here for assisting in finding lost items. We should try it." She read the words and everyone repeated them. Erin did her best to believe that spells and such really worked, but it was hard. She'd not been raised to believe in such things. Although her mother was a free spirit, her parents had attended a non-denominational Christian church all of Erin's life.

After three tries of repeating the spell, they sat in silence. Erin looked up at the ceiling and then studied the crown molding, hoping for inspiration, but nothing came to mind. She let out a breath, then thought of something that caught her by surprise.

Erin jumped to her feet. "I'll be right back. I remembered something."

Once in her bedroom, she opened the wardrobe door and reached up and pulled a small weathered box that she'd had since just before her paternal grandmother's passing. For some reason her grandmother had insisted Erin keep it, telling her one day one of the items within would come in handy.

Already ill, her grandmother had asked to speak to both Erin and Aubrey. She'd instructed them to get the box from under her bed. Then she'd told them to guard the contents, that one day something in the box could save them.

Gone were the days of spending time with their exuberant grandmother who took them on holidays, extravagant parties at beautiful locations. A vibrant woman, with not only a great sense of style, but quite the beauty, she was always on invite lists.

She'd died soon after that day, when giving them the box. Aubrey had insisted Erin take it and they'd one day open it together. But time had passed, and they'd put it off. Perhaps too afraid to revisit the raw with grief of her passing.

Returning to the front room, she sat and held the box in her lap. "I'm sure there is nothing in here like a dagger. My grandmother gave Aubrey and I this box and I've never looked inside. I suppose this is the time to see whatever she insisted I needed to have."

While the others looked on, she untied the ribbon that was wrapped around the box, the soft fabric sliding from her fingers. Lifting the top off the dilapidated container, her eyes widened. There was a neatly tied stack of one-hundred-pound notes.

"That would have been nice to have while I was at university," she quipped.

There was a small framed picture of her grandparents. Both looked to be younger than her own twenty-eight years. The young couple held hands and gazed shyly at each other.

Not wanting to get emotional, she put it on the seat next to the money.

"Looks as if the rest are letters and ... oh a fan, a handkerchief and ..." Erin lifted the items and gasped. Under everything was a small sheathed dagger, its intricately designed golden handle inscribed with the initials ETM, Her grandmother's initials.

Edwina Therese Macguire.

Why had her grandmother owned a dagger? That wasn't something Erin would have ever guessed. Why in the world had she required one?

When she lifted it from the box, the others exchanged looks. Tammie beamed. "You are the key. You will save them all."

Erin swallowed. "Oh goodness."

Chapter Eighteen

The men had finally sat down to a hearty meal of the roast boar Tristan and Gavin had killed, potatoes from the cabin's overgrown garden and cheese they found stored in the larder. Padriag found it increasingly difficult to eat past the lump in his throat every time he looked around the table to the men with whom he'd eaten many a meal over the last centuries.

"I fortified the wards," he finally said. "My magic is stronger since I returned."

Niall cut off a chunk of cheese and placed it on his plate. "My healing powers seemed enhanced. I think we are all stronger in our gifts. It must be something conjured by our partners' spells."

Tristan who had the power of strength lifted his arms and flexed. "Stand behind me in battle lads. I will protect you."

Everyone gave him a droll look, except for Liam who nodded as if agreeing. "We will need all of our strength for what comes ahead. I suggest that we spend the time eating and resting. The final test will come soon."

"In your vision," Padriag began, "do you see the battle here or elsewhere? Do you remember the surroundings?"

"I saw a stone wall behind us. I believe it is taller than this cottage," Liam replied.

Niall spoke next. "Erin saw herself looking out of a window to us beneath. So I think it could be elsewhere. The keep perhaps?"

"That is what I was considering," Padriag added. "Her description of the dreams brought the keep to mind. If it were Meliot's castle, she would have mentioned the darkness and you Liam would have also felt it."

But that made no sense. Why would they return to a vulnerable place that Meliot knew well? It had been their sanctuary for centuries and although Padriag wanted to return to where he considered home, it was much too risky.

"Let's give it a few days," Tristan said. "We need to practice swordplay. It has been long since I held one."

The men opened bundles they'd brought from the modern world then changed into leather breeches and tunics they'd bought from someone in the village who made authentic costumes for a local Renaissance Fair held every year.

Gavin twisted at the waist, sword up at chest level. "These clothes are much more comfortable than the ones we wore in the sixteen hundreds."

"Not the same without some sort of vermin crawling

over them at night," Padriag stated and held his sword up. "Stop delaying your defeat, Gavin."

Just as the Scot raised his sword, his gaze flicked past Padriag, his grip tightening. "A woman comes," he murmured, his voice edged with unease.

Padriag turned to see her—a tall, gaunt figure moving toward them. She wore a tattered black dress that trailed behind her like a shroud, the fabric dragging on the ground. Her gait was unnatural, her steps uneven yet deliberate, as if there was a planned destination in mind. She did not falter at the sight of five armed men.

Tristan stepped forward, his hand on his hilt. "Is someone following her?" His voice was wary. "Something is... wrong."

Niall's expression darkened as he took a step closer. "Could be a witch."

The woman halted just feet away, her lips curling into a sneer. Her skin was pallid, mottled with patches of gray, death clinging to her. Sunken eyes—dark, unreadable—fixed on them. She was an unnatural contradiction of ageless yet ancient.

"Honorable men wouldst help a sick woman," she rasped, her voice a hoarse whisper. "Or do you intend to harm me instead?"

A chill coiled around Padriag's spine as her gaze locked onto him. A predator assessing prey. He exchanged a glance with Tristan, his fingers flexing at his side.

"I'll ward myself and speak to her. Stay here." He handed his sword to Niall but kept his daggers across his chest.

As Padriag stepped forward, the woman tilted her head, studying him as if peeling him apart with her stare.

"What is it you require?" he asked, keeping his voice steady.

Her eyes narrowed. She did not answer at once, her attention flicking past him to the others. Then, at last, she exhaled a slow breath. "I am quite hungry."

The words had barely left her lips before her body convulsed. In an instant, her face contorted, her mouth stretching unnaturally wide, her jaw unhinging. Her torso elongated grotesquely, bones cracking as she grew taller, her limbs distorting into something monstrous. Dark gray scales broke through her skin. Her fingers lengthened into grotesque claws, wickedly curved talons gleaming in the sunlight.

Padriag stumbled back, cursing himself for not having his sword.

The men lunged into action, Niall tossing Padriag his sword. He caught it, pivoting into a defensive stance as they formed a semicircle, blades raised, muscles coiled for battle.

The creature reared onto its hind legs, throwing back its horned head. A screech tore from its gaping mouth, a piercing, bone-rattling cry that sent a tremor through the ground. When its gaze locked onto them once more, its mouth parted to reveal rows of serrated teeth, each one honed for the kill.

And then—it charged.

Snarls and screeches split the air, a cacophony of rage and menace that seemed to echo. The sound crawled into their bones, reverberating through the ground making it shift under their feet. But there was no room for hesitation.

The five men surged forward, swords gleaming under what was left of the suns' light, their minds sharpened to one singular purpose—kill or be killed.

There was no doubt about the creature's intent. It had been sent to destroy them, to strike before the prophecy could come to pass.

Towering and monstrous, the beast was a walking terror. Every inch of it bristled with death, from the jagged fangs lining its grotesquely stretched mouth to the talons curving like sickles from its gnarled hands. Its tail, long and wickedly spiked, lashed across the ground with lethal precision that promised a gruesome end to any man who miscalculated his step.

But Padriag and the others were no strangers to seemingly undefeatable threats. This was not the first abomination they had faced—though it was among the most formidable. They had survived before. They would persevere again.

A surge of energy flooded through Padriag, a strange, tingling sensation crawling beneath his skin like spiders weaving a web through his muscles. His body tensed, readying itself for the battle to come. He rolled his shoulders, drawing that strange power inward, harnessing it as he steadied his grip on his sword.

The moment the five men clashed with the beast, their blades moved with deadly precision. Metal sang as it sliced through the air, each man executing swift, precise strikes meant to cripple or kill.

Battle cries tore from their throats, echoing through the trees, with the ancient war calls of their clans, defiant and unyielding. They fought, not as separate warriors but as one, their movements synchronized from years of battle, an unspoken brotherhood forged in blood.

The creature lunged, its spiked tail whipping toward them like a barbed whip. Padriag barely had time to react, leaping over the deadly appendage as it slashed across the ground, carving deep furrows in the dirt. He twisted midair, thrusting his sword downward, aiming for the beast's flank.

The blade struck true but bounced off the armored scales, skidding uselessly as though striking stone.

A curse hissed through his teeth. Their weapons were all but useless against its thick hide. Their strongest blows left nothing but shallow chips, as if they were trying to fell an ancient oak with a rusted dagger.

Then a breakthrough.

Tristan lunged, his sword slipping beneath the edge of a scale, burying deep into the beast's side. The creature let out a bone-rattling yowl, its massive claw swiping blindly. The force of the strike sent Tristan hurtling backward, his body crashing into the earth with a sickening thud.

"Under the scales!" Gavin bellowed, driving his own blade into the creature's other side before leaping clear of the retaliatory swipe.

Razor-sharp talons raked across the warriors, tearing through fabric, biting into flesh. Blood slicked the ground, but still they fought. They had no choice but to endure.

The beast shrieked, a piercing, mind-numbing sound,

and spun in a violent circle. Its tail lashed out, this time striking high, level with their chests.

Padriag had no time to react. The brutal impact sent him flying sideways, his body slamming into a tree with a force that shook the branches. He crumpled to the ground with a groan of pain.

But there was no surrender in him.

Fueled by fury, he forced himself upright, shaking off the pain. His vision sharpened, his breath steadying. With a raw, guttural battle cry, he surged forward once more, his sword raised, his sights locked onto the beast.

This fight was far from over.

The fight against the creature became harder when it took to the air and dove down over their heads, its talons outstretched as they swung their blades in what seemed a fruitless effort to defend themselves.

Padriag rushed to Tristan. "I have an idea." Leaning closer, he pointed to the cottage and explained.

Giving a nod, Tristan raced toward the building as the rest of them distracted the beast. Moments later, he and Tristan climbed onto the roof. Padriag nodded toward Tristan and his friend crouched down.

"Hey ugly, over here!" Padriag called out getting the creature's attention. Immediately, it changed course flying directly toward him.

Padriag stood at the ready, his gaze locked on the beast. They had to time it perfectly, their plan would only work if Tristan was precise.

They had only one chance.

Its great wings flapping, front and hind legs outstretched the creature prepared to grab Padriag, its intent clear. It would fly high and drop him to his death.

It drew closer and closer until Padriag felt the wind generated by its wings. Yet he stood still, waiting, keeping his breathing steady.

As the claws lowered, Padriag threaded his fingers together as Tristan rushed forward and used them as a springboard. Using every ounce of his power of strength, Tristan thrust his broadsword upward, cutting through the softer underbelly, slicing it open. Both men fell backward, landing on their backs.

The beast let out a monstrous screech circling over as its guts spilled over them. Then it plummeted through the air and skidded across the ground, leaving a trench of black blood.

Those on the ground cheered, and Padriag looked down on the bloodstained trio in torn clothes and couldn't help the swell of pride that blossomed in his chest. They'd conquered so much since being thrust into this world, had lived through unimaginable torture, survived and mourned the passing of their families. Through it all with one common goal, to one day break the curse and if at all possible, destroy Meliot. And now, here they were in these final hours, fortified by the enhancement of their power and the strength that came from knowing there were people on the other side that were not only waiting for them but also providing help in whatever way they could.

Tristan lay on his back, his gaze pinned on the darkening violet sky. "You know what Padriag?"

"Hmm?"

"I fucking hate purple."

Padriag chuckled. "Come on, let's get down. We need to ensure the beast is truly dead."

Chapter Nineteen

The spell book remained open on the coffee table, notebooks next to it as well as crystals, pouches and other paraphernalia that they hoped would be useful. The main question besides how the dagger that was the key to breaking the enchantment was to be used, was how they would get it to the alter-world.

Erin eyed the small blade once again and let out a weary sigh. The sun was setting, marking the end of a long day.

John was on the floor, on his stomach, leafing through pages of an old book. Gwen sat in a chair holding a crystal on a chain and softly chanting. Sabrina and Tammie were at the kitchen table, speaking softly and scribbling notes.

The most Erin had contributed was ordering take out and finding the dagger. She had no idea what else to do as she didn't have even a speck of imagination when it came to the mystic arts.

She glanced around her flat noting the weariness on

everyone's faces. Understandable because it was unthinkable to give up. There was too much at stake.

Knocks on the door announced the food delivery and she opened the door to find not only a young man holding two large bags, but Aubrey as well. Her cousin took the food from the young man and walked past Erin, who held out a generous trip.

"Take a break people," Aubrey announced as she walked into the flat. "I have an idea, but I need you all fed and refreshed before I share it."

Everyone exchanged startled looks, even Erin, who'd not told Aubrey about her visitors.

PLATES PILED high with all sorts of Chinese dishes, the group sat down, eating and exchanging thoughts. Erin leaned over to Aubrey.

"How did you know we were here?"

Aubrey shrugged. "I tried to call you, and when you didn't answer, I called your Mum. She did the location thing and told me you were here."

"She can do that?" Erin asked incredulous since her mother barely knew how to use her own phone.

"I helped her set it up when you were dating that creepy guy, Dan. In case he took you or something."

"I shouldn't be on their plan. I'm an adult, but Dad insists on paying for it. It makes him happy." Erin smiled despite finding out her mother had the ability to track her every move. "Dan was different, but he wasn't creepy."

"I disagree," Aubrey insisted. "He had serial killer vibes."

John cleared his throat. "What is this idea of yours Aubrey?"

Her cousin took a long drink from her tumbler which was probably filled with her favorite Scottish soda, Irn-Bru.

"This may be farfetched, but what if you summon the scary blond man and ask him what is happening over there?" Aubrey suggested.

The room was silent. Although the idea had merit, they didn't trust the man, Gunther.

"I am not sure we can summon him," Sabrina said.

Tammie shook her head. "And not to mention he is enslaved by Meliot, one of his minions."

"Can't trust him," John said. "If he talks about us to the wizard, it will hinder everything we are doing."

Erin was torn. She believed Aubrey's assessment that Gunther seemed to genuinely want to help, but at the same time, it was true he worked for Meliot.

"When I was taken to the alter-world, Gunther was there. He stood between me and those horrible creatures when I was taken to the room. I am not sure what they meant to do to me, but they turned away and left when he wouldn't budge," Erin said then shrugged. "Unlike everyone else, he never threatened me."

"But he did take you there, both you and Tammie. It was he who came here and followed Meliot's orders," Gwen reasoned. "I am not sure we should trust him."

Tammie held her hands up. "I admit, he was reluctant to turn me over to those ugly creatures, but in the end he didn't put up much of a fight and let them take me."

Standing, Sabrina went to the kitchen and returned with

another serving of food. "What if we summon him and ask him questions? We can cast a truth spell and see what happens."

John became animated, rubbing his hands together. "That is not a bad idea,"

Everyone turned to look at Aubrey, who slid a glance toward Erin. "What?"

Erin shrugged.

"It should probably be you, Aubrey, who summons him," Gwen informed them.

Aubrey's eyes rounded like saucers. "Oh no, I just had the idea. I am not into any of this." She made a circular motion with her right hand. "That man was huge and scary and he's probably a bad guy." She stood. "Know what, bad idea. Very bad idea."

"Remember the box grandmother gave us?" Erin asked.

Aubrey slowly nodded.

Letting out a breath, Erin lifted the small dagger. "This was in it. Aubrey, it's possible that we are meant to be part of this. Have been meant to be here all along."

Aubrey reluctantly reached for the blade and inspected it. "Grandmother had this?"

This time it was Erin who nodded. "Yes and remember what she said that an item in the box would someday help us, or something like that."

"I will stay, but only because of this. And I prefer not to summon him." Aubrey handed the dagger back to Erin.

Erin herself was nervous at the idea of seeing Gunther once more, but she would face him again if it meant helping Padriag.

"He is not that scary. But he is huge and a bit off-putting," Tammie said.

"Off-putting!" Aubrey exclaimed. "That is putting it mildly."

John motioned to Aubrey. "Perhaps your presence will be enough. If you could just assist, it would be helpful."

Lowering to sit, Aubrey squeezed herself between John and Gwen. "Very well, but I am not going to talk to him. In case he tries anything, I'm hiding behind the biggest person." She gave John a sweet smile. "Have no doubt, I will sacrifice you in a minute."

"I do not blame you," John replied and stood, straightening to his full height. His voice carried quiet authority as he spoke. "Tammie, Gwen, Sabrina, and I will form a protective square around the room. Aubrey, sit outside the circle. Erin, stand next to Gwen—she has the strongest magic."

As they moved into position, John, Gwen, Sabrina and Tammie took a deliberate stance, hands outstretched, forming an unbroken chain of power. Their murmur of ancient words filled the air, the chant rhythmic and steady. Erin's skin prickled as a chill raced over her arms, and she exchanged a glance with Aubrey, who sat rigid, her eyes wide with fascination.

Then, the air shifted. A breeze stirred, unnatural and deliberate, sending Erin's hair fluttering around her face. In the center of their formation, shimmering particles of silver light spiraled, twisting until forming into a denser shape. A heartbeat later, Gunther appeared.

He looked around the room with confusion, his ice-blue eyes scanning the room, his scarred face tight. He stood barefoot, clad only in breeches, a damp cloth clutched in his hand, evidence they had pulled him from whatever mundane task he had been tending to.

A deep frown creased his brow as his gaze swept over them, lingering the longest on Aubrey. For a moment, he simply stared at her, something unreadable flickering in his sharp eyes before he growled, "What am I doing here?"

Erin couldn't ignore the imposing sight of him—broad shoulders taut with muscle, his torso crisscrossed with old battle scars, each one a testament to a life of suffering. The most striking of all was the jagged mark running from his brow down to his jaw. Somehow, rather than diminishing his handsome face, it only made him more formidable. With his near-white blond hair and those piercing, glacial eyes, his Dutch ancestry was undeniable.

Gunther's expression darkened as he took a step back. "I cannot be here."

"We need your help," Erin stated firmly.

Tammie folded her arms. "Consider it repayment for kidnapping us."

Gunther's gaze flicked back to Aubrey before he exhaled slowly. "I cannot help you."

"Why not?" John pressed. "There is no other way to get a message to our men."

Sabrina tilted her head, watching him closely. "Do you not wish to redeem yourself?"

A muscle in Gunther's jaw flexed. "There is no redemption for me." He let out a slow, measured breath. "I should return before I'm missed."

Aubrey stood then, moving toward him, her expression

pleading. "I know it's dangerous. I know you risk being caught. But we only need one small thing delivered."

Gunther tilted his head back, as if searching for strength in the ceiling's beams. "What is it?"

"This," Erin answered, producing a dagger and holding it out. "We need it to reach Padraig."

His gaze dropped to the weapon, then rose to meet hers, his expression unreadable. But then, his voice came low and grave. "You should know—the attack is imminent. They will not survive. Their time has run out." He gestured toward the dagger. "That will change nothing."

Silence fell over the room, heavy and suffocating. Erin's chest tightened as dread curled inside her. She slid a look to Gwen who's eyes shone with unshed tears.

Still, Erin lifted the dagger higher, her voice unwavering. "Take it. Even if it doesn't change the outcome, we have to try."

For a long moment, Gunther didn't move. Then something flickered in his eyes—pity, perhaps, or reluctant understanding.

"Very well," he murmured. "I will try."

He reached for the dagger, and the moment his fingers closed around the hilt, he vanished with a swirl of lights.

Erin released a shaky breath and let her shoulders sag. "He'll get it to him. It has to work."

No one answered. Slowly, they returned to their seats, the weight of uncertainty settling over them like a heavy shroud. There was nothing left to do but wait—wait and pray for the survival of the five brave knights.

Chapter Twenty

As the keep loomed in the distance, an unsettling sensation slammed into Padraig, his chest constricting. It wasn't fear. It was certainty. His body and mind knew this was to be the last time he would stand inside the ancient walls. Either he would leave and return to the other realm … or he would take his final breath here, among the ruins of the home that had defined him for centuries.

The others must have felt it, too. No words were spoken as they dismounted the aurochs, the massive beasts stamping their hooves against the dry, cracked earth. They stood in a silent line, shoulders squared, gazes locked on the once-mighty fortress that had sheltered the knights through times of despondency, fear, injuries, healing, and time itself.

Liam and Tristan took the aurochs toward the remnants of the stables at the far side of the keep. The creatures, despite their formidable size, were docile, their deep, wary snorts breaking the brittle silence.

Padraig couldn't blame them for their unease. This place was nothing like their native plush Esland. Here the land was a barren husk, swallowed by extremes, searing heat by day, frigid cold by night.

The front door of the keep hung open, swinging slightly on rusted hinges. It wasn't surprising. They had fled in the heat of battle, leaving the stronghold vulnerable.

Beyond the threshold, devastation awaited. The front room, once grand and welcoming, was obliterated. Splintered wood and piles of ash covered the floor, the remains furniture reduced to charred ruins. Animal tracks crisscrossed the soot-covered stone floors, evidence of creatures that had sought warmth here in their absence.

Swords in hand, the men inspected every inch of the keep. Only after every corner was deemed safe did they relax.

"We should barricade ourselves inside for the night," Tristan said, returning from the stables hauling a massive wooden plank from outside.

Gavin moved toward the hearth, uncovering a broken-handled broom and brushing away layers of cold ash. "I'll get a fire going. It should help drive out some of the chill."

Rushing upstairs, Padraig found several blankets that had survived the destruction and carried them down to place on the floor in front of the hearth.

They moved through the motions, each man taking on his task without need for discussion.

Tasks completed, the five sat around the growing fire in quiet concentration, fashioning crude spears from broken beams, whittling the ends to deadly points and hardening them in the flames.

Padraig finished one and tossed it onto an ever-growing pile. "Liam, any idea when Meliot will attack?"

"Not yet." Liam frowned, running a hand over the rough grain of a newly carved spear. The Brit shook his head and tossed another weapon to the pile of spears before disappearing into the darkness of the upper levels, needing silence to surround him when he summoned visions.

Niall finished sharpening a spear and turned his attention to the kettle, lifting it from the fire's iron hook. "I'll boil water. We should have something warm before taking shifts sleeping."

Years ago, when they had still harbored hope of reclaiming their lives, they had fashioned a hand-pumped well in the back room of the keep. It had been their lifeline, allowing them to gather water even when it was too dangerous to venture outside. Now, it was one of the last remnants of their preparations.

Padraig searched the kitchen shelves, fingers brushing over dust and emptiness. There was nothing, no food, no provisions. Only a few brittle sticks used for making tea. He crushed a few between his fingers, inhaling the sharp blend that reminded him of cinnamon.

By the time Liam returned, each man sat with a cup cradled between his hands. Niall silently poured another cup and held it out.

Liam took it, but his expression was grim. "They come. They will arrive at dawn."

The men exchanged looks, but there was nothing that needed to be said.

"There is something else," Liam added, his fingers tightening around the warm metal of the cup. "Something unexpected will come. I tried to see, but something is blocking me."

No one spoke for a long moment.

Then Tristan exhaled, his broad shoulders easing as he glanced around the ruined hall. His gaze softened, though his voice was strong when he finally spoke.

"In a way, I'm glad this is ending—no matter the outcome." His eyes moved from face to face, lingering on each of them. "We have fought, endured, and survived for longer than any man should. And now, as we stand on the edge of fate, I can say with pride; I could not have chosen better men to stand beside me."

Padraig's throat tightened. Something in his chest clenched hard and fast. He swallowed against it and nodded. "Together, we conquer."

A roar of agreement filled the hall, their voices rising as one.

"Aye! Aye!"

They lifted their cups in unison, a final toast to battle, to brotherhood ... to the end.

The men settled around the hearth to sleep. They would need as much rest as possible before facing whatever the next day brought.

A SOUND like thunder shattered the silence.

Padraig's eyes flew open, his pulse slamming in his chest as he pushed up from where he'd slept beside the dying hearth. Across the room, Niall stood watch, motionless by the window, his silhouette rigid against the pale moons' light creeping into the ruined keep.

Padraig's voice was hoarse. "What is it?"

Niall didn't turn. "I see the light of torches. The sound could be horses."

Padraig was on his feet in an instant, crossing the floor in three strides. On the horizon, lines of fire flickered in the distance. The torches bobbed and swayed in waves, their golden light stretching across the darkened landscape. Meliot's army. Hundreds of soulless creatures moved steadily closer.

A sense of anticipation filled Padraig. The suns would rise soon, and with them, clarity. What they faced would be evident, whatever the outcome this would be the last day of the life they'd known.

Behind him, the other knights were already moving.

Liam and Tristan fastened their leather harnesses, each loop filled with sharpened daggers, their movements swift and practiced. Liam slung two bows over his shoulder, disappearing up the ruined staircase to the upper floor where he would have the best vantage point. With over a hundred arrows, Padraig had no doubt the Brit would take down more than his fair share of enemies.

Padraig turned toward the rickety table where his own weapons lay. His fingers moved swiftly, securing the belts across his chest and hips, the familiar weight of steel pressing against his ribs somewhat soothing.

Then came the sound.

Womp. Womp. Womp.

The air vibrated as a dragon's wings cut through the

sky. The night collapsed into day in an instant. Unlike the world they'd once known, this realm had no gradual dawn—just a sudden, searing light that forced temporary blindness until the eyes adjusted.

Padraig squinted through the brightness. The torches had stopped. A ripple passed through the approaching army. They were disoriented, blinking against the abrupt shift from night to day.

A smirk tugged at the corner of his mouth. Idiots.

He shoved open the front door, just wide enough to crawled through and going forward until he could hide behind the tangled branches of a bush. The ground trembled beneath him, a dull, rhythmic quake the unmistakable thunder of hooves closing in. Through the dense branches, he watched them near

He lifted his hand. A ball of fire flickered to life in his palm, spinning and twisting, growing hotter with each moment.

When the first wave of horsemen crossed into the trap they'd laid the night before, he let the ball of fire fly.

The flames struck.

With a roar, fire exploded across the dry brush, racing outward in a wave of destruction as the wall of fire circled the keep. Horses reared, their riders thrown as the inferno swallowed everything in its path. The screams of burning men filling the air, a horrifying symphony of agony.

Padraig wasted no time. With a flick of his wrist, rings of energy formed in his palms—discs of concentrated power. He flung them one after another, cutting through the chaos, severing limbs, knocking dark warriors off their mounts, sending more bodies into the roaring flames.

It didn't take long before his arms began shaking from exhaustion, still he continued. This was a chance to take down as many as possible.

Suddenly, a heavy hand shoved him back.

"Go! I'll handle it," Gavin barked, stepping forward.

Padraig knew better than to argue. He scrambled back as the giant Scot lifted both arms, palms outward. An arc of raw energy formed, humming with power. He unleashed it.

Lightning-fast bursts shot through the second wave of Meliot's army. Those not caught in the blasts were picked off one by one by Liam's arrows, each shot clean, deadly, unerring.

The keep's front courtyard was filling with corpses sprawled among the smoldering remains, arrows piercing skulls, spears jutting from still-twitching bodies.

Still, they came.

Niall and Tristan stepped forward, forming a deadly line. Their spears struck true, taking down what remained of the advancing force.

Padraig closed his eyes, pulling every ounce of strength he had. Shimmering domelike barriers formed, wrapping around his friends like an invisible wall. It would hold. For now. But he knew—Meliot's power was stronger. The shields would not hold against him.

A new tremor shook the ground beneath his boots.

"We'll hold here. Go check the rear!" Tristan called out over the din.

Padriag raced into the keep and raced upstairs to a crumbling balcony. A bow and quiver waited there. He grabbed it.

Some of Meliot's men had managed to make it past the fire and were advancing.

The dark warriors were trampling over their own fallen to breach the back defenses.

The others had to defend the front where there were more opponents

The arrows Padriag had wouldn't be enough. There were too many enemies.

Fire. It had to be fire.

Summoning another ball of flame, he hurled it downward.

The second line of brush ignited.

Screams erupted, the smell of burning flesh filling the air.

Padriag grabbed the bow, notched an arrow, and fired. Another. Another. Each shot found its mark, thinning the herd of whatever creatures had survived the flames.

At last, the rear of the keep fell silent.

Breathing hard, he hurried back to the first level, where the others had returned inside and peered out through the cracks in the stone.

"Where is the dragon?" Padriag asked.

Liam, stood by a window peering out. "Circling. It's not attacking—it's scouting. Probably sending messages back to Meliot."

"At least there's only one dragon," Niall muttered. "That we know of."

They had little time to waste. The men rushed outside, reinforcing their firewall with more dried brush, oil, and powder before retreating into the keep to drink water and prepare for what came next.

THEY BARELY HAD time to catch their breath before Tristan's voice rang from the top of the keep.

"I see sentinels! More fighters incoming!"

The wolf-creatures were formidable.

Padraig's stomach clenched. Unpredictable. Ruthless. And worst of all—fast. They couldn't wield swords, but the creatures' teeth and claws were just as deadly.

The battle raged again.

They triggered the fire—more screams, more bodies turned to ash. Arrows and spears rained down, Niall and Tristan's spears finding their marks.

Then—the ground trembled.

A third wave thundered toward the keep.

Overhead, the dragon shrieked, and fire rained from the sky.

They barely made it inside before the ground where they'd stood was scorched black.

Through the window, Niall cursed. "Centaurs."

Padraig's gut turned to ice. Elite warriors. Eagle-eyed. The centaur archers were death itself.

His jaw clenched. "Gavin, time to test those shields."

How much longer could they hold them off?

Padraig had no answer. But as he crouched behind the crumbling wall, watching the dust and smoke on the horizon, he knew one thing.

This was only the beginning.

Chapter Twenty-One

Exhaustion weighed heavily on the five knights, their breath coming in ragged gasps as they exchanged grim looks. Blood, dirt, and sweat streaked their faces, but Padraig still managed a sharp grin. "Time to use what we have left and kick some ass."

Liam's quiver lay empty, his daggers long spent. Only two spears and his sword remained. Niall gripped his last two daggers, his knuckles white, his sword hanging at his side. The rest had nothing but their blades, their hands blistered and bleeding from the endless fighting.

Padraig's arms ached from keeping the shields of protection in place, the shimmering barriers flickering, growing weaker with every passing second. Gavin, though he still summoned energy blasts, swayed slightly, his huge body betraying his exhaustion.

Only Tristan, with his supernatural strength, stood steady, his stance unwavering. But even he could not defend them alone.

Then came the sound that froze the blood in their veins.

A thunderous boom shattered the air and seconds later, the front of the keep exploded inward. The only redeeming factor was when the boulders they'd set on the roof's edge tumbled from above, smashing into the enemy below with bone-crushing force. A final set of boulders dislodged from the roof, flattening those unlucky enough to be caught beneath them. But the brief satisfaction of taking down a portion of the enemy force faded instantly.

Through the gaping hole, the full horror of their situation came into view.

Lines of Meliot's mounted warriors stretched as far as the eye could see, their dark-armored forms gleaming under the suns' light. Interspersed among them, centaurs stood at attention, muscles rippling, bows at the ready. Their presence alone sent a fresh wave of dread crashing over Padraig.

Then, as one, the warriors parted. A figure moved through the ranks with measured, deliberate steps. Meliot.

The warlock's robes billowed around him, his black eyes gleaming with triumph. A slow, mocking smile curled his lips.

"I must commend you," he said, his voice laced with cruel amusement. "An entertaining fight, indeed. But surely, you see there is no victory for you." He gestured to the waiting army behind him. The sheer number of them overwhelming.

His smirk widened. "Surrender, and I promise you a quick, painless death." His gaze roamed over each of them, lingering on their grimy faces. "Your curse is nearly at an end." He tilted his chin toward the heavens. "Three moons will shine down in mere moments. And then—you will be mortal."

"You have not won yet," Tristan called out, defiant. "We will die in battle before we let you take pleasure in our surrender."

Meliot chuckled, a hollow, chilling sound. "Quick death or die fighting—it matters little to me." He lifted his arm. "Once I give the signal, all will be over for you." His grin stretched, grotesque in the flickering torchlight. "Thank you for the centuries of ... keeping me entertained ..."

Womp. Womp. Womp.

The deep, rhythmic beating of wings rumbled overhead.

Meliot's grin faltered. He turned his gaze upward, confusion flickering across his features. Then, a shriek tore through the sky. His dragon—his own beast—appeared, an orange glow along its blue-black scales ... and then, in an instant, it was engulfed in flames.

A roar of agony split the air as the massive creature plummeted, its body consumed in a raging inferno before slamming into the earth with a deafening thud.

Meliot spun in a circle, searching the heavens with wild eyes. His army hesitated, awaiting his command.

Padraig felt it then—a surge of power, like an electric charge crackling beneath his skin. He flicked a glance at Gavin, who met his gaze with a barely perceptible nod.

Raising his hands, Padraig summoned the last of his energy. Strips of fire and light wove together, curling and twisting like snakes.

As one, they struck.

The energy wrapped around Meliot, tightening like

chains of steel. The warlock let out an angry scream unable to do more than struggle with his arms pinned to his sides.

"Get them, you fools!" he shouted at his minions.

The enemy surged forward—only to be met by a wall of flame.

Beautiful dragons with scales of green, blue, and lavender, burst into view, their sinuous bodies twisting in the sky. They roared in unison, their calls sending a tremor through the battlefield. With graceful, deadly precision, they rained down fire, incinerating everything beneath them.

Centaurs fired arrows skyward, but they fell short. Nothing could touch the winged giants.

"Where did they come from?" Gavin asked, his voice barely audible over the chaos.

Padraig laughed as the ground rumbled beneath them. "Esland." His grin widened. "The Eslanders have arrived."

Hell itself broke loose.

Eslander warriors charged into battle atop massive aurochs, their colossal mounts moving with terrifying speed. The great beasts plowed through Meliot's forces, crushing everything in their path. Swords shattered against their thick hides, arrows bouncing harmlessly away.

Padraig fought to keep the bindings around the wizard strong, but he was tiring.

Veylen, the leader of the Esland army burst through the fray, his ice-blue piercing gaze locking onto Padraig. "I brought you a gift."

Three aurochs were brought forward by Esland warriors. Tristan, Gavin and Niall mounted whilst Liam went to fetch the two in the stables.

With renewed hope, the knights atop the great beasts stormed into the fray.

The hold on Meliot burst and the wizard disappeared.

"Meliot," Padraig said to Gavin.

"He is weakened and won't go far," the Scot replied.

Atop the auroch, Padraig searched among the fighters for the wizard.

The battlefield was a frenzy of clashing steel, screams, and the thunderous pounding of hooves.

But Padraig barely noticed. His focus was on one man.

Meliot.

He turned and looked toward the keep. If the wizard was truly weakened, then he could have sought refuge.

His pulse spiked.

"I'm going after Meliot," he told Liam.

Liam's jaw tightened. "Be careful. His magic is still strong."

Sword in hand, Padraig urged his mount away from the battle to the front of the keep and leapt from the saddle, his feet sure on the scorched ground. He barely paused before striding inside, sword at the ready, his heart hammering.

He spotted Meliot near the remnants of the hearth, his hands raised, lips moving in a frantic whisper. A spell.

"You will never be free." The wizard called out.

Padraig stepped fully into view, his grip tightening on his sword. "You're weakened. You can't flee, can you?"

The warlock's sneer deepened, his black eyes narrowed. "I remain more powerful than you will ever be."

With a flick of his wrist, Meliot sent a blast of energy crashing into Padraig, sending him sprawling.

Pain ignited through his ribs, but Padraig fought through it, rolling to his feet. He shot a disc of fire in retaliation. Meliot staggered.

"You're not so sure anymore, are you?" Padraig taunted.

The warlock's face twisted in fury. With a sharp motion, Padraig's sword was yanked from his grasp. It hovered midair—then turned, its deadly tip aimed at him.

Padraig barely had time to curse before the blade shot forward. He dove, hitting the stone floor hard as the sword embedded itself on the wall behind where he'd just stood.

Another blast sent him slamming into the wall. He gasped for breath, struggling to rise.

As the wizard walked closer, Padraig struggled to all fours.

Meliot yanked the sword from the wall and stared down at Padriag. "I won't grant you last words." He brought up the sword, but then abruptly stopped. "What do you want?"

His stomach tightened, as Gunther appeared. Was the guard there to help Meliot?

Gunter walked in with purposeful steps. "Our forces are failing. You must leave before they overcome us."

Taking advantage of Meliot's distraction, Padriag scrambled to stand. The guard's gaze barely flicked to him, but he didn't warn the wizard. "You must leave, my lord."

"I have something to see to first. Then we leave." Meliot turned to face Padriag a satisfied look on his face. "Are you prepared for death?"

A flash of gold caught Padriag's attention, the guard tossed something to him. Padriag caught it mid-air. It was a golden dagger.

Meliot glanced over his shoulder to his warrior.

Time seemed to still, every movement in slow motion. The dust in the air flowed at a meandering pace. Silence enveloped them.

First quiet, then louder, Erin's voice echoed in his ears, it was as if she stood there in the room, it was so clear.

"By love unbroken, by bond unshaken,
I summon the heart that fate has taken.
By moon's soft glow and sun's first light,
Break these chains, undo the night.
Through endless time, through veil and mist,
Let not our bond be lost, dismissed.
By whispered vow and promise sworn,
Return, this knight, from where he was torn.
From shadows deep and silent grave,
Rise once more, be strong and brave.
By fate's design and heart's decree,
The knight's return will come to be."

In an instant, the silence shattered—the sounds of battle crashing back into the world.

Meliot spun, hands raised, fingers curled like claws, and with a terrifying screech he lunged at Padriag only to gasp his black eyes widening.

The golden dagger was buried deep in his chest.

The warlock staggered, his trembling hands reached for

the dagger's hilt. "Wh-where did you g-get it?" His voice was weak, breathless.

"My fairy Dutch mother."

Meliot's body swayed—then collapsed. His lifeless eyes open. As malevolent magic left him and floated in the air, it surrounded Gunther, who stood stock still. After a moment, the mist dissipated and both men let out a breath.

"Thank you," Padriag managed.

The guard gave Padriag a nod, glanced at the dead warlock and walked out.

Chapter Twenty-Two

The air seemed to leave the room and Erin sat up in bed, the darkness enveloping her. Her dream had been so vivid. Padriag was battling Meliot, and the wizard was stronger. At a loss of how to help, she'd heard a woman's voice clearly.

"The spell. Speak it out loud."

She'd repeated the words over and over until giving up on sleep.

It was still dark outside, but she was too restless. If she was meant to help, she had to be awake. Slipping from the bed, Erin went to the kitchen opened the refrigerator and peered inside.

"Wine," she whispered. "Come to mama."

After uncorking the bottle, she poured a glass and padded to the front room. Not knowing what happened in the alter-world was torturous.

If the five men didn't return, it meant they were either

dead or trapped forever. Lost to this world, never to see their homeland again.

An errant tear trailed down her cheek and she didn't bother wiping it away. Through all the turmoil and confusion of the last weeks, she'd somehow managed to form a bond with Padriag. Picturing not ever seeing him again was crushing.

It wasn't love, not yet, they'd not known each other well enough, but in her heart, there was no arguing with knowing that he was her person. The man she could easily fall in love with and spend the rest of her life with.

So many times she'd heard the quote, "When you know, you know," and she knew, there was not a single doubt in her mind. Why did it have to be a man with so many complications, a man who'd been alive centuries before her?

Her lips curved. He was positively the most devastatingly handsome man she'd ever known. With rugged looks, Padriag was pure man. Despite his tortured past and the cursed kingdom he came from, he was brave and positive. He'd managed to adapt to the changing times, which was admirable. Every single one of the five knights were men of incomparable courage.

The air shifted, circles of tiny lights swirling in the air. Erin eyed the glass of wine. "What the hell?"

The swirls became denser, and she braced for what would happen next. If it was Gunther, she had no weapon to use against him, unless tossing wine in his face worked. Erin backed up slowly, moving toward the kitchen and the one sharp knife she owned.

A scream caught in her throat when a ragged figure

appeared, his face covered in soot, clothing torn and bloodied.

"You helped me, you were there." Padriag had appeared, unsteady on his feet, but with a wide grin. "We did it, we're free." The last word caught in his throat.

"Oh my god," Erin took a step toward him and placed her glass of wine on the table. "Are you injured?" She wasn't sure where to touch him as every inch of his skin was either black from soot or caked with dried blood.

His mouth opened and before he could utter a word, he toppled sideways and passed out.

"Oh no," Erin rushed closer and tapped his cheek. "Padriag. Padriag." From the bedroom, the phone's ringtone sounded but she ignored it. "Wake up."

The ringing stopped as she leaned over Padriag to see if he was breathing. He was, and his pulse was strong.

The cell phone began again.

Erin rushed to her bedroom. Not so much to answer the call, but to call for an ambulance. She'd figure out a way to explain his clothing and condition once he was no longer in danger.

Tammie's name flashed on the screen, and she tapped on the green circle to answer.

"Is Padriag there?" Tammie called out, obviously on speaker phone. "The rest of the men are here. They did it," her voice caught. "Is he there? Please tell me he is there."

"Stop talking and let her answer," Sabrina's voice sounded closer to the phone. "Erin, Padriag didn't show up here."

Erin let out a shaky breath. "He is here, but he passed out. I think he's injured. I was about to call nine-nine-nine."

"Do not call anyone," Tristan's voice came over the speaker. "He is not injured. Any blood you see if probably not his. He needs rest."

"Liam passed out as well," Tammie called out. "He's coming too now."

Erin was back at Padriag's side. His eyes were open, and he blinked in her direction. "Where's everyone else?"

"At the castle," Erin replied watching as he sat up. "Ouch," he rubbed the side of his head. "I banged my head pretty good."

"Padriag," Tristan's voice returned. "Stay there and rest. We can all gather tomorrow to talk."

Once the others were assured that Padriag was safe and that Erin agreed to let him stay the night, they ended the conversation.

Erin met Padriag's gaze. "I am so glad. You did it." She reached for him, but he held his hands out.

"I don't want to get whatever all this crap is on you. I need to wash up," Padriag said. "Then I will kiss you properly." With a devilish grin, he winked at her. Erin couldn't help but chuckle at how funny he looked with a dirty face and disheveled hair.

"I have clothes here for you. The others brought it when they came here in case you came here. They must have suspected you might since this is your ancestral home." Her cheeks warmed, when she considered that perhaps the others thought Padriag would appear here because of her.

. . .

An Unlikely Knight

WHILE HE SHOWERED, Erin made herbal tea and toasted bread. When he emerged, she had a plate of buttered toast and jam waiting, as well as the tea

Wearing a simple blue t-shirt that clung to his muscular build and jeans hanging low on his hips, Padriag looked as if he belonged in modern times. His damp hair fell in lazy waves to his shoulders, framing his stubbled jaw and clear hazel eyes.

Padriag padded barefoot to where she sat and, without hesitating, he leaned over and kissed her fully on the lips. His mouth lingered over hers until her eyes fell closed and she reached up and slipped her hand around his nape, wishing to deepen the kiss.

By the time he straightened, her heart was thumping so hard she was sure it was audible.

"Please eat. Tell me what happened," Erin said motioning to the toast. "I don't have much more to cook right now. Everything would take too long."

He sat in the chair next to hers and met her gaze. "Thank you. I am very hungry. With the difference in days and time, it hard to know how long it has been since I've eaten."

Between bites he told her everything. How they'd defeated the first wave of Meliot's army. The wizard's appearance and how, just when they thought defeat was eminent, Esland had come to their rescue.

It was a fantastical tale that kept Erin breathless. Each turn of events, the creatures involved, and the medieval forms of battle kept her glued to every word. When he finally described how Meliot died, Erin gasped.

Erin spoke in a soft reverent tone. "My grandmother's

dagger was the key to your freedom. I can't believe it. How can that be possible?" She closed her eyes needing a moment to consider what it could mean.

"What is it?" Padriag asked.

"If the dagger was a way to end the wizard, the fact my grandmother had it, could only mean one thing."

Padriag's gaze dropped, and he reached for her hand. "What do you think it means?"

"That my grandmother must have been to the alterworld. Or someone she knew came from there. How else would she have an ancient item from that realm?"

He nodded and took another sip of tea. "There are many people in this world that have traveled to other realms. I am sure of it."

"I will never know. But I do wonder the reason for her insisting I have the box of what seemed to be inconsequential items."

Erin let out a long sigh. "So many questions about everything. I suppose we have to be accepting that we may never know all the answers."

Standing up, Padriag let out a long yawn. "I can barely keep my eyes open. Can I sleep in your bed?" He held out his hand and Erin took it.

They slipped between the sheets and Padriag pulled Erin close. Within moments he was fast asleep.

It was after midnight, she wasn't sure of the time as she lay in his arms. It would take years to describe how she felt in that moment. One day she and Padriag would tell their children the tale of how they met, it would be a fairy tale that perhaps they'd grow up to not believe. It wouldn't matter, because as long as she and Padriag lived, the adventure would remain with them always.

Upon waking, Padriag breath came in short shaky gasps. He fought the roller coaster of emotions, doing his best not to break down. It was true. He was free, it hadn't been a dream.

It was early, the dim sunlight slipping through the space between the curtains.

Erin lay on her side, lost in sleep, her breathing slow and even. Her features were bathed in that gentle light. Her full, pink lips were slightly parted, her long, light brown hair spilling like silk across the pillow, catching the glow in warm strands.

She was breathtaking.

He could spend years watching her sleep. It was difficult to swallow past the growing emotions, a mixture of happiness and excitement. How had he come to be there, not only free, but with such a woman?

Just being near Erin brought him peace, settled his errant thoughts. Any idea that he was unworthy, or that he did not belong there, evaporated when she touched him. Somehow, he had to come up with a way to tell her how deeply he felt for her. That life without her in it was unthinkable. Just thinking that she didn't feel the same way scared Padriag more than facing the hundreds in battle.

When she opened her eyes, she gave him a sleepy smile. "Have you been watching me sleep?"

"I have. You're beautiful."

She leaned forward and kissed him. It was a soft and sweet. "Some would say it's creepy."

"I want to wake up every morning like this, looking at you."

When she reached for him and pressed her body against his, Padriag was immediately lost in her.

They made love with the desperation of two lovers finding each other again, their bodies joining with passion so strong it enveloped them completely.

Erin's husky moans and calling out his name filled him with need, with want, with a sense of purpose as they raced toward the peak that would not only shatter their souls, but bond them in a way only lovers understood.

Their cries of release intermingled as they floated, clutching onto each other as their bodies shuddered and trembled.

Erin recovered first. With an expression of a well-satisfied woman, she raked her fingers through Padriag's hair. "You are so very special to me."

Her words made his insides warm. "I cannot fathom being with anyone else."

A shadow crossed her face, and she searched his eyes for a long moment. "Padriag, you have to take time for yourself. It is important that you spend time getting your bearings, figuring out what you actually want to do. As much as it would break my heart, it would be selfish of me to expect anything from you.

He rolled onto his back bringing Erin to lay over him and looked into her eyes. "I have been waiting three hundred years for you. I know without a doubt you are the woman I want to be with."

Everything within him seized, waiting for her reply. It was too much to hope for. That Erin would feel the same soul-deep longing that had gripped him the first time he'd seen her. Not for one second had he tried to push feelings for her away. The pureness of love was the one thing he could never deny, not after so many years without expecting anything beautiful in his life.

"I want to tell you something," Erin replied, and his heart stopped. She was about to let him down gently. He almost laughed, there would be nothing gentle about it.

Her cheeks blossomed pink, and she pressed her forehead against his. Finally she lifted her eyes, searching his. "I have no doubt that you are the man for me. I can't believe I'm saying this, but ... I am yours Padriag Clarre. My entire heart and soul are yours."

Tears sprang to his eyes as her words seeped into his mind, skin, body. Pulling her tightly, he kissed Erin's temple. "Thank God."

Chapter Twenty-Three

Two weeks later.

Sunlight spilled over the bustling streets of Edinburgh. It was the perfect day for a walk—an outing Padraig had insisted upon, eager to immerse himself in this modern world he was only beginning to grasp. Holding Erin's hand as they strolled along the busy sidewalks was something he had only dreamed of for so many years that he'd long since lost count.

Every time their reflections passed in the polished glass of storefronts, he had to do a double take. There they were, an ordinary couple among the throngs of city-goers, laughing tourists, and chattering locals. Their fingers entwined as if they'd been walking like this forever. To anyone who passed by or lounged on park benches, they were nothing more than another couple enjoying a beautiful day.

But for Padraig, this was nothing short of a miracle. This was the first time he had ever truly planned a day on his own. Not just existing, not simply surviving, but living. Interacting with shopkeepers and making mental notes of trinkets to buy, sights to revisit, landmarks to explore. Every moment felt like a treasure.

The city was alive around him. The scents of fresh bread from nearby bakeries, the tang of roasting coffee, the murmur of conversations, and the constant hum of traffic blended into a thrilling symphony. Yet it was all so overwhelming. Several times, Padraig had to stop, his chest tightening as he drew deep breaths, willing his thundering heart to calm.

Erin's gentle hand in his always brought him back to himself, her quiet understanding grounding him in ways he could not put into words.

"We should head to the castle," Erin said, her voice like a soothing balm that steadied him. She cradled a small bag filled with treasures from a quaint stationery shop: a pair of journals, stacks of vibrantly printed papers, pens of every imaginable color, and two elegant fountain pens.

During breakfast, she'd come up with the idea of creative journaling. As they walked, she snapped pictures of his every interaction, her smile growing whenever he marveled at the smallest things—like the sleekness of a touchscreen or the uninhibited affection of a dog that had barreled toward him, tail wagging wildly, oblivious to its owner's shouts.

On a side street, Erin paused to admire trinkets through a shop's window. A soft smile on her lips that lingered made his chest tighten.

"I have enjoyed these days with you, getting to know you better," Padriag said, earning a warm look. "I love you Erin

Maguire." He had to swallow past the lump in his throat. "Please, don't say anything."

"Are you okay?" Erin asked, searching his eyes..

"Not really," Padriag took her by the shoulders. "Erin. I do not have much to offer, but in this moment, I want to ask that you find a place in your heart for me."

"Oh Padriag, you already own my heart. I love you." She cupped his chin with her hand. "I love you Padriag Clarre."

When he went to speak, to remind her that he was penniless, she interrupted. "We will work out the future. For now, I want to continue forward. You're meeting my mother and her husband, we are going to see about a bigger place to live, perhaps Ashcraig Hall. There is the matter of figuring out how to get you a current identity."

"We better get to the castle, we'll be late as it is." She took his hand, tugging him gently and he gladly came alongside, his heart lighter.

Once they were settled in the car, she turned to him, her cheeks still pink from the briskness of their walk. "Are you ready?"

Padraig nodded, the tightness in his chest easing at the warmth of her gaze. He knew she wasn't just asking about joining the other men at the castle. She was asking if he was ready to step away from the alter-world, to allow himself to truly live in this one.

They wound through the twisting roads of the village of Culross, its picturesque beauty tugging at something deep within him. Thatched-roof cottages and charming stone houses passed by like remnants of a half-remembered dream.

He recalled this place from his long-ago visits to Castle Dunimarle when he often came to spend time with Tristan.

The castle's imposing silhouette came into view in the distance, a grand relic of the past still clinging stubbornly to the present. His pulse quickened at the sight of it.

"Can you stop the car for a moment?" he asked, his voice rough.

Erin pulled the vehicle to the side of the road and killed the engine, watching him with those keen, perceptive eyes. Padraig climbed out and walked to the front of the car, his gaze sweeping over the sprawling landscape.

It was breathtaking, the way the castle stood proud against the endless sky, surrounded by a sea of lush greenery and jagged cliffs. It hadn't changed. Not really.

"What's wrong?" Erin's voice came softly from behind him. She slipped her arm around his waist, her touch as steadying as it was reassuring. "It's beautiful, isn't it?"

He swallowed past the sudden tightness in his throat as he scanned the area before him. "I am really here, I live here now."

Erin stepped away, her presence a quiet, supportive comfort. She understood him so well, her instinct to give him space confirming she was his perfect partner.

Finally, Padraig returned to the car and closed the door behind him. He glanced at Erin, a smile of determination lifting his lips. "We best get there."

A CELEBRATION SOUNDED on the castle grounds, a lively buzz of laughter and music floated in the balmy air. Tristan's "aunt," Edith McRainey—who was, in truth, his descendant—had arrived with her nephew Derrick McRainey, a young man Padriag had met only once before.

Beneath a broad canopy, a long table groaned under the weight of lavish platters brimming with fresh fruits, roasted meats, and decadent pastries. Glass domes shielded the dishes from greedy flies, their gleaming surfaces reflecting the golden light of the afternoon sun.

Musicians strummed fiddles and plucked guitar strings, the cheerful tunes adding to the festive feel.

For the first time he could remember, Padriag saw his friends relaxed, their faces creased with unguarded joy as they swapped stories and playful barbs.

"Padraig!" Tristan waved his friend over. "I was beginning to think you'd decided not to come."

Padraig grinned, his eyes gleaming with amusement. Erin rose to her toes and kissed his cheek before stepping away. "Go," she urged him, her smile soft. She drifted toward the shaded cluster of women gathered beneath the branches of an ancient tree, their greetings sounding happy.

Adjusting to seeing his friends in modern clothing was still a struggle for Padriag. They seemed at ease in the new clothes, except for Niall, who looked like he was ready to claw his own skin off.

"Is something wrong?" Padraig asked, unable to hide his smirk when Niall fidgeted and tugged at the waistband of his trousers.

"Too many layers," Niall grumbled. "Why do people wear clothing beneath these cursed pants?"

Padraig's laughter rang out, rich and hearty. "You don't have to. Some men prefer not to."

"That's good to hear," Niall said with a scowl before stalking off toward the castle's entrance, no doubt to relieve himself of the offending undergarments.

THE DAY PASSED in a pleasant blur of music and merriment continuing until the early evening. After the musicians took their leave, Edith and Derrick said their goodbyes and followed suit.

Moments later, Gwen, Erin, Sabrina, Tammie and John busied themselves gathering the remnants of the feast to take inside, leaving the five friends alone as the sun began to dip toward the horizon.

"I need to speak with you," Tristan said, his gaze steady on Padraig.

"Of course." Padraig's stomach tightened, sensing something weighty in his friend's tone.

"Come." Tristan gestured toward a grassy rise from where they could overlook the surroundings.

The two men walked to the higher ground and stood quiet as the now cooler breeze brushed against their faces. Padraig's gaze swept over the rolling hills and plush flatter grounds.

"I remember when we rode here as lads," Padraig said, his voice thick with nostalgia. "Not a care in the world."

"Aye." Tristan's smile was tinged with sadness. "We were so irrationally carefree back then. Thinking life would be like that always."

Padraig glanced at his friend, noticing the way Tristan's jaw tightened, his expression as unreadable as the sky. He waited, letting the silence do its work.

"I am grateful my family kept my lands, even expanded the borders. You and the others are my family now. It is only right that I share what I have with you. The lands have been equally divided between the five of us."

Padraig's mouth opened, but Tristan's expression left no room for argument. "It's legally done, so you cannot refuse it. Oh and my lawyers have taken care of everything, you are a legal resident of Scotland, whose birth was never recorded by your now dead parents."

A rush of emotions surged making it impossible for Padriag to speak.

"Miraculously, coffers of gold, that I put in a hidden cave below the wine cellars were still exactly where I left them," Tristan continued, his voice raw with emotion. "It's been converted to currency and deposited in accounts under each of your names. For as long as you live, you will be comfortably wealthy."

Padraig's eyes shimmered with unshed tears, and his throat tightened. "Tristan, this ... You didn't have to—"

"It's because of me." Tristan's voice cracked. "Because I insisted we attend that cursed assembly of knights. Because of me, we lost everything. I have to repay my debt."

Padraig shook his head. "It was not only your fault. I was the one who demanded we go to defend the village. I led us to confront Meliot's guards that day bringing the curse upon our heads."

Tristan huffed a reluctant laugh. "Very well, we're both

to blame. Don't tell the others, aye?" His lips twitched with the hint of a smile. "Gavin, Niall, and Liam agreed to wait until you were here. As a group, you will choose which lands to claim as your own."

Emotion thickened Padraig's voice as he clasped his friend's shoulder. "Thank you, Tristan. For everything."

Tristan pulled him into a fierce embrace, their friendship unbreakable in the passage of centuries.

A loud clearing of throats interrupted them, and they both turned to find Gavin, Liam, and Niall standing nearby, their gazes drawn to the sprawling land below.

Side by side, the five men stood in silence

No words were needed.

They'd finally come home.

Epilogue

Aubrey let out a weary sigh as she parked the car in front of Ashcraig Hall, the car's old engine rattling like it shared her frustration. Despite its temperamental quirks, she enjoyed driving the 1992 MG her father had gifted her when she'd gone off to university.

After hours of haggling with the city council for permission to build her yoga studio in the nearby village, her nerves were fraught. But tonight was her reward—wine, snacks, and mindless television. Pure, blissful nothingness.

She wrestled grocery bags from the boot of the car and trudged into the house, her footsteps muted by the thick rugs.

Once everything was put away, Aubrey changed into pajama pants and a hoodie. In thick socks she padded into the sitting room with a tray of meat, cheese, and fruit.

A huge orange tabby cat she'd named Oscar was already there, sprawled across a throw pillow like he owned the place. An up-until-recently stray, Oscar's mismatched eyes—one gold, the other a cloudy gray—lifted in her direction before he turned his jagged-eared head away with royal indifference.

"Nice to see you too, Oscar," Aubrey murmured, shaking her head with a fond smile. She'd found him in the village, a scrawny, filthy creature following her with a determined loyalty she couldn't shake.

A few vet visits, baths, and a steady diet later, Oscar still looked like a feral mess, albeit a much fatter one. But he'd made himself at home.

"Oh darn, I forgot my glass of wine," Aubrey groaned, tossing her hands up in frustration. She spun on her heel and made her way back to the kitchen.

A scream tore from her throat as she stumbled backward.

Gunther stood in the middle of her kitchen, his broad frame seeming to shrink the space. His face was grim, carved from stone, and his icy blue eyes locked onto her with unsettling intensity. A sword gleamed in his hand, its edge wickedly sharp.

"Wh-what do you want?" Aubrey's voice was a broken whisper, her gaze darting between his towering form and the deadly weapon. "Are you here to kill me?"

For a heartbeat, Gunther's expression softened, the coldness in his eyes replaced by something unreadable. "No. I am not here to kill you."

Aubrey's throat tightened. "Kidnap me, then?" Why on earth was she giving him ideas?

Gunther's massive shoulders rose and fell in a slow, measured breath, his blond hair brushing his shoulders like a golden curtain. "No. I have come to speak to you."

"Me?" she squeaked, her fingers trembling as she edged toward the keys hanging by the back door.

He nodded, his gaze pinning hers. "Aye ... er, yes."

"Uh ... okay. Why don't you pour us some wine then?" She forced herself to sound calm, to act like her entire evening hadn't just taken a terrifying turn. If he was pouring wine, his hands wouldn't be on that sword.

Except, of course, he slid the weapon into a scabbard across his back with the ease of someone who'd done it a thousand times. Her stomach twisted as he poured wine into a glass and another into a simple cup for himself.

"As I am responsible for Meliot's death, his cursed magic now fills me." His voice was flat, resigned, like he'd been sentenced to something he already accepted. "The dark realm is mine now."

Aubrey's mouth dropped open. "What? Why would you want that?"

"It seems I have little choice in the matter." His gaze dropped, and for a moment, the towering, intimidating man looked ... afraid.

"There's always a choice," she replied softly. "Can't you just stay here?"

His eyes lifted, something raw and aching swimming in their depths. "I cannot leave the other realm for long. I am cursed. Like your friends were. But I am the last knight."

"Cursed?" Aubrey's breath hitched. "The others broke their curses. Since you helped them, I'm sure they'd help you break yours."

A dry, humorless laugh escaped him. "The only way to

break my curse is for someone else to take Meliot's place. I will never leave that forsaken realm."

The sadness in his voice twisted something inside her. "What can I do to help?" The words slipped out before she could stop them, and Aubrey groaned inwardly. Why was she trying to help him? He'd broken into her house, for crying out loud.

"I am beyond redemption and do not deserve to be saved. But I came to speak to you because I saw you in Meliot's book. I believe he may be your sire."

"Ha!" Aubrey barked out a laugh. "I think you've got your wires crossed. My mother is from Ghana, and trust me, she's conservative as they come. If there was some magical affair going on, she would have had something to say about it."

"There are ways," Gunther said, his tone grave. "Magic does not always play by the rules of man."

A shiver crawled down her spine along with memories of her mother often telling her stories of strange dreams while pregnant with her. Aubrey shook her head. Nope, not possible.

"Look, thanks for the wild story. And congrats on the ... uh, job promotion. But you should go back and get on with doing evil deeds or whatever you plan to do."

Gunther met her gaze. "Where is the dagger?"

"I don't have any idea, and I don't care."

The man let out a long breath. "It has been safeguarded by your family for a very long time. Ensure it is protected."

"I will pass the word," Aubrey said waving a hand toward the back door. "Please leave."

Gunther's eyes narrowed as if she'd challenged him. And then, with a nod, he said, "I will see you again. It is inevitable."

And just like that, he vanished. One moment there, the next, gone. Leaving behind a faint, earthy scent of crushed leaves and damp forest air.

Aubrey's legs felt like wet noodles as she stared down at the glass of wine she'd been gripping like a lifeline. Did that just happen?

Her gaze fell to the cup he'd poured himself, still sitting on the counter, untouched.

What did he mean by seeing her again being "inevitable?"

"First thing in the morning, I'm calling Erin." Aubrey clutched the wine bottle to her chest like it was a shield.

She glanced toward the living room where Oscar remained soundly asleep, entirely indifferent to the chaos she'd just endured.

"Some guard cat you are," she muttered and took a long swallow, then refilled her glass.

Tonight, she would forget about Gunther and his ominous warnings. Tomorrow ... find out what secrets her grandmother had kept, how her family was involved and, why was Gunther back.

Also by Hildie McQueen

The Cursed Kingdom

An Enchanted Knight

A Beautiful Knight

The Darkest Knight

An Unlikely Knight

Clan Ross

A Heartless Laird

A Hardened Warrior

A Hellish Highlander

A Flawed Scotsman

A Fearless Rebel

A Fierce Archer

Clan Ross of Skye

The Wolf

The Hawk

The Raven

The Falcon

Guards of Clan Ross

Erik

Torac

Struan

Clan Ross of the Hebrides

The Lion

The Beast

The Eagle

The Fox

The Stag

The Duke

The Wildcat

The Hunter

The Bear

Rogues of the Lowlands

A Rogue to Reform

A Rogue to Forget

A Rogue to Cherish

A Rogue to Ensnare

Historical Scottish Novellas

Declan's Bride: A Highland Romp

Ian's Bride: A Highland Rom 2

The Lyon's Laird

Medieval Highlander Romance: The Seer

Pirates of Britannia

The Sea Lion

The Sea Lord

Laurel Creek Series

Jaded: Luke

Brash: Frederick

Broken: Taylor

Ruined: Tobias

Brides for All Seasons

Christina

Sarah

Wilhelmina

Aurora

Lucille

Esther

Scarlet

Isabel

Montana Cowboys

Montana Bachelor

Montana Boss

Montana Beau

Montana Bred

Montana Born

Montana Born & Bred

SHADES OF BLUE
Big Sky Blue
A Different Shade of Blue
The Darkest Blue
Every Blue Moon
Blue Horizon
Montana Blue
Midnight Blue
Shades of Blue Boxed Set
Blue Montana Christmas

HISTORICAL WESTERN ROMANCE
Judith, Bride of Wyoming
Patrick's Proposal

WESTBOUND SERIES
Where the Four Winds Collide
Westbound Awakening

THE FORDS OF NASHVILLE
Even Heroes Cry
The Last Hero
Nobody's Hero

THE MORIAG SERIES

The Beauty and the Highlander

The Lass and the Laird

Lady and the Scot

The Laird's Daughter

Highland Medieval Romance

Highlander - The Archer

The Duke's Fiery Bride

Contemporary & Western Romance

Melody of Secrets

Taming Lisa

Cowboy in Paradise

About the Author

***USA Today* bestselling author Hildie McQueen** brings action, romance, and unique settings to life in her captivating stories. From sweeping Scottish historical romance to thrilling contemporary romances, her books offer something for every reader to devour!

When she's not weaving tales, Hildie loves diving into a good book, connecting with fans at events, exploring new places, and spending time with her three adorable pups. She lives in the charming small town in Georgia with her superhero husband, Kurt, who makes every day an adventure.